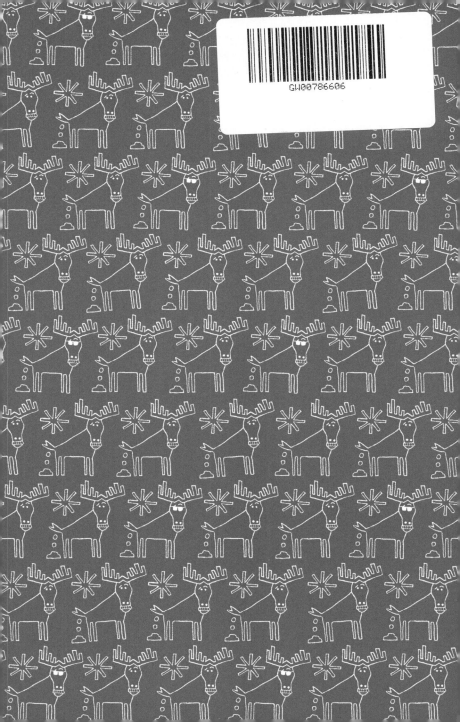

GW00786606

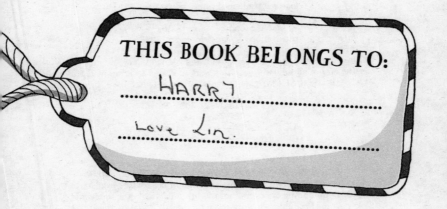

THIS BOOK BELONGS TO:

HARRY

Love Lin.

Published in the UK by Scholastic, 2023
1 London Bridge, London, SE1 9BG
Scholastic Ireland, 89E Lagan Road,
Dublin Industrial Estate, Glasnevin, Dublin, D11 HP5F

SCHOLASTIC and associated logos are trademarks and/or
registered trademarks of Scholastic Inc.

ISBN 978 0702 33082 7

A CIP catalogue record for this book
is available from the British Library.

Printed and bound in Great Britain by Clays Ltd, Elcograf S.p.A
Paper made from wood grown in sustainable forests
and other controlled sources.

MIX
Paper | Supporting
responsible forestry
FSC® C018072

1 3 5 7 9 10 8 6 4 2

www.scholastic.co.uk

STEPHEN MANGAN

THE GREAT REINDEER RESCUE

ILLUSTRATED BY
ANITA MANGAN

SCHOLASTIC

OTHER FANTASTICALLY FUNNY BOOKS BY STEPHEN AND ANITA MANGAN:

For my nephews and nieces:
Cy, Danny, Leela, Maddie,
Noah and Rohan.

CHAPTER ONE

This was his first Christmas working as one of Santa's reindeer, so Dave was nervous. And when Dave was nervous, he talked too much.

"Ooh, look at that Christmas tree!" he exclaimed to no one in particular. "I've never seen one with pink flashing lights before! I might do my tree like that next year. I like pink lights. You don't see them that often, do you? Pink lights? They're tremendous. So pink! And light! I normally have white lights on my Christmas tree or sometimes lots of different colours. But never pink. It never even occurred to me to have pink lights! Funny!"

The other reindeer said nothing. They weren't being deliberately rude but were simply concentrating on what they were doing — flying Santa's sleigh at great speed through the night sky. It took huge effort. Dave understood this and wished he could stop talking. But the more he wanted to stop talking, the more he talked. He couldn't help himself.

"My mum made a fairy for the top of our

tree one year," he said. "It was a reindeer fairy, of course. It had cute antlers and wings and a sweet red bow around its neck. I made a little umbrella for it because it looked like it might *rain, dear!* Get it?! Reindeer – rain, dear! Ha! Ha! Ha! Ha! Ha! Ha!"

No one else laughed. It had started to snow heavily, and it was becoming difficult to see where they were going. Dave still couldn't stop talking. He had so many questions!

"How come we can fly tonight?" he asked. "I can't fly the rest of the time."

"Santa harnesses the power of starlight and gravity using his magic box," said Comet, the powerfully built but softly spoken reindeer next to him.

"Will I be able to fly tomorrow too?" Dave asked.

"Christmas Eve is the only night we fly," Comet said.

Comet's parents had called him Comet because on the night he was born they'd seen a comet tearing across the sky reflected in his huge eyes. "That's how much we loved you, Comet," they used to say to him. "A rare comet appeared and we didn't even turn round to look at it. We couldn't stop staring at your big, beautiful eyes." It was a story that brought him to tears whenever he remembered it, but he never mentioned it to any of the other reindeer. Comet was extremely shy and much more sensitive than was expected from such a big and strong reindeer.

Comet faced forward again, concentrating on running hard. Dave wondered whether Comet found him annoying or wished he'd stop talking. To be fair, Dave also wished that Dave would stop talking, so he tried to.

He really tried hard. There were a hundred things he wanted to know, but he bit his lip.

He lasted about thirty seconds, and then he couldn't take it any more.

"**Dasher?**" he called out to the reindeer behind him. "**How come we can go so fast when our hooves have nothing but air to grip on to?**"

There was no response. Dave tried again but louder.

"**DASHER? HOW COME WE CAN GO SO FAST WHEN OUR HOOVES HAVE NOTHING BUT AIR TO GRIP ON TO?**"

"**I heard you the first time,**" said Dasher dreamily. "**I was just thinking about how amazing it would be if I were a rockstar,**" because I'd be so rich and famous I wouldn't need to work and I could lie around doing nothing all day."

"If anyone round here is going to be a rockstar," said Rudolph, the reindeer at the front, "it's ME!"

"No, yeah, Rudolph, sure," said Dasher. "I'd love to be famous like you."

"No one will ever be famous like me," said Rudolph. "I'm Rudolph."

"Yes, you are," said Dasher. "You are Rudolph. Totally. You're the most famous. You always will be."

Rudolph snorted and tossed his head as if to say *this conversation is over*.

In the silence that followed, Dave was wondering whether to ask Dasher his question again when Dasher said, "So, yeah, right, Dave.

You want to know how we can run so fast on air? It's all the dark matter in the universe. Dark matter is stuff that's there, but you can't tell it's there and you can't see it or feel it, but it's really there and we're running on it. Got it? Good. Now I'm going back to my rockstar daydream."

Dave hadn't really got it, but he didn't say so. It was difficult being the new one in the group. The reindeer he had replaced was Blitzen, who had retired last year. Blitzen couldn't run as fast as he used to, so Santa had gently suggested it was time for him to call it a day. Dave had got the job, much to the delight of his parents. Being one of Santa's reindeer was a sought-after position; Dave knew how lucky he was and was trying hard not to blow it.

Best not to ask any more questions, he told himself.

He lasted fifteen seconds.

"Cupid?" he asked, picking a different reindeer to bother. "Why don't we stop on the roof of every house?"

"You have to, like, think about it for one second," drawled Cupid, slowly batting her incredibly long eyelashes. Cupid was very beautiful; other reindeer were always falling in love with her. "If we stopped on every roof on the planet, it would take sooooo long. We'd never be able to deliver presents to all the children in the world. It would take, like, aaaaages. Can you even imagine? Booooooring! So we zip at top speed down every street and over every house, and Santa is able to slow down time using his magic box—"

"He can *slow down time*?!"

"Yes!" exclaimed Cupid. "Don't ask me how, but he slows down time just for him so that he can run around doing loads of things in, like, a blur. I have no idea how it works. Seriously, I'm absolutely hopeless at that stuff, but as we fly over a house, he slows down time so he can jump off on to the roof, climb down the chimney, deliver the presents, eat and drink anything left out for him, maybe leave a note saying thanks, perhaps have a little nosy around (I bet he has a little nosy around – I would, I soooo would), then climb back up the chimney and hop on to the sleigh, all in less than the blink of an eye."

"That's why no one ever sees Santa delivering presents," said Dancer, the reindeer wearing a headband and legwarmers in the back row. "He slows time down for *him*, but to the rest of us it all happens in a flash. I worked it out: Santa takes about a thousandth of a second to deliver presents to one home. So he delivers presents to one thousand homes every second! That's *fast*!"

Dave had kept confusing Dasher and Dancer with each other to start with because their names were so similar. He kept calling Dasher "Dancer" and Dancer "Dasher" until he realized that Dancer actually *was* a dancer. She loved ballet. When they weren't pulling Santa's sleigh, she was constantly doing warm-up exercises and stretches. Dasher, on the other hand, was nothing like his name. He never wanted to dash anywhere unless it was into bed to go to sleep. Dasher was easily the laziest reindeer Dave had ever met.

Donner, the reindeer with generous teeth

and an eyepatch in the back row next to Dancer, told Dave of the awful year when Santa's magic box had broken halfway across Russia.

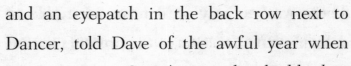

"We set down at the edge of a forest next to a family of confused Russian bears, and Santa got to work on the magic box. We were all panicking.

There was no way we'd have been able to deliver even a fraction of the presents in time without that magic box. It really looked like we'd have to cancel Christmas. I'd never seen Santa so stressed. Turned out Dasher had put some cheese sandwiches and a packet of crisps in the bottom of the magic box, thinking it was a cool box!"

"WHY ARE WE TALKING ABOUT THIS?" shouted Dasher. "The magic box looks exactly like a cool box, so it wasn't my fault."

"Santa was so angry," said Donner, ignoring him. "He's normally pretty red in the face, but this time he looked so red I thought he might pop."

"Let's not tell that story again, shall we?" said Dasher.

The reindeer fell silent once more as they

swooped at incredible speed over rooftops. Dave thought how amazing it would be if the other reindeer grew to like him and became his friends. Imagine Rudolph being his friend! And Cupid! Then he wondered what would happen if they all decided they *didn't* like him, and they complained to Santa about him talking all the time, and if Santa then fired him and Dave was sent home and he'd have to tell his parents and how disappointed and upset they'd be with him. Dave started to panic about this happening. He *had* to stop talking so much. But the nervous panic he was feeling made him want to talk even more.

"How can this sleigh carry enough presents for all the children in the world?" he blurted out.

"Santa has a carefully worked out route

that passes across different storage centres," answered Prancer, a reindeer with large eyes full of wonder and curiosity and antlers painted silver. "It's amazing. As the sleigh flashes over them, it's loaded up with more presents. The preparation for Christmas takes all year."

Dave was surprised to hear this. He thought Santa just threw a load of presents into the back of the sleigh and set off. There was, it turned out, far more to it than that.

Rudolph, at the front, snorted and tossed his head again. He didn't like the conversation not being about him.

"Yeah, I'm Rudolph," he said to Dave, even though Dave already knew that. "Santa tells me I'm the best reindeer he's ever had, and I believe him. I'm amazing. I'm fast, I'm strong, I've got a great sense of direction, I look wonderful, my hooves are the shiniest, my coat is the smoothest, I'm the most hydrated reindeer of all time and even my farts smell like perfume. You're going to love working with me, Derek."

"My name's Dave."

"Sure. So watch and learn, Derek. Watch and learn."

Dave had to admit that Rudolph was indeed fast and strong. You had to be if you were the reindeer at the front. Rudolph had to set the pace and be able to gallop all night. If he slowed down, everyone else would slow down, and they'd never get all their deliveries done in time. And if he took a wrong turn at any point then the whole schedule would be thrown off course. Santa was too busy jumping on and off the sleigh with presents to steer it – that was down to Rudolph. He was an incredibly important part of the team, but didn't Rudolph know it!

As the sleigh tore through the night sky, flying fast and low over houses and blocks of flats, rivers and lakes, cities, towns and villages, Rudolph sang his favourite song loudly and tunelessly. It came as no surprise to anyone that it was a song he'd written himself.

I'm number one,
I'm number one,
That's why I'm at the front,
And you're looking at my bum.

CHAPTER TWO

Holly could not get to sleep. She lay in her bed and stared at the ceiling. There were two reasons why she was finding it so hard to nod off.

First of all, it was Christmas Eve. Tonight was the night she'd been looking forward to for *months*. In fact, she'd been looking forward to it since Boxing Day last year. Holly *loved* Christmas. If it were up to her, she'd have Christmas every week. That would be the best thing ever.

It wasn't just the presents that she loved, although, come on, who doesn't like presents?! Holly loved absolutely everything about Christmas. She loved fairy lights. She loved Christmas trees. She loved being the one to put the fairy on the top. She loved Christmas carols and listening to them while sitting under a blanket in the living room with a mug of hot chocolate. She loved getting presents and she loved buying gifts for others.

She loved all the sweets that suddenly

appeared around Christmas time, and she loved hiding a stash of them in a shoebox under her bed, then helping herself late at night or first thing in the morning. When else do you get to eat chocolates so early in the morning?!

She loved that normal rules about going to bed were relaxed at Christmas, and that often she got to stay up late and no one seemed to notice. She loved that there was no school and she loved seeing her cousins and her aunts and uncles.

She loved looking at the presents under the tree and trying to work out what they were. She loved Christmas Day food. She loved waking up to find that Santa had been. She loved Christmas movies. She loved playing games and she loved trying to do the thousand-piece jigsaw that her dad always started on Christmas Eve, even if they rarely finished it.

She loved Christmas cards arriving in the post. She loved hearing stories about past Christmases, and how one year everyone had been excited to give her a toy car that she could sit in and pedal around, but after she'd unwrapped it Holly had been more interested in playing with the box it had come in than playing with the actual present.

She wasn't the only one in the family who loved Christmas so much. Her dad, Simon, loved Christmas maybe even more than Holly. And her mum, who died when Holly was small, had loved Christmas more than both of them put together.

After all, her parents had loved Christmas so much they had named her Holly Anthee Ivy Carol Noelle Eve Mary Angelica Gabrielle Mistletoe Tinsel Zuzu Smith.

The two names that most confused people were *Anthee*, which her dad had just made up so that her first three names sounded like "Holly and the Ivy", his favourite carol; and *Zuzu*, which was the name of the daughter in her mum's favourite Christmas movie *It's a Wonderful Life*.

Christmas had also made Simon famous in their town.

Their house wasn't particularly big or unusual. It looked like all the other houses on the little cul-de-sac on which they lived. But it stood out at Christmas. It stood out so much that people travelled from miles around to have a look at it. Some nights there might be five or six cars outside with people taking pictures.

What caused all this fuss? Holly's dad's Christmas displays.

They got more extravagant every year. He put up Christmas lights all over the outside of the house and garden. This year there were about three thousand lights! There were strings of lights along the line of the roof. Lights around every window. Lights around every door. Lights wrapped around the chimney.

There were twelve illuminated Santas climbing up the walls. In the small front garden there was an illuminated Nativity scene, fifteen illuminated reindeer, snowmen, elves, Christmas trees and one big sleigh. There was barely a square centimetre of space on the front of the house or in the front garden that wasn't lit up by colourful flashing lights. It looked incredible.

This made for a wonderful Christmas display, but it also meant that Holly's bedroom, at the front of the house, was even more brightly lit at night than it would be in the middle of a summer's day. Holly liked one small light on when she slept, but this was like trying to sleep next to the surface of the sun!

She loved the lights, but she wasn't the only one who found that they made sleep difficult. Many of their neighbours had complained over the years, especially Mr and Mrs Throat-Badger who lived across the road.

"My wife," Holly's dad had insisted, **"loved those lights. She loved Christmas and so do we. They are a tribute to her. We'll NEVER stop putting lights up at Christmas. NEVER!"**

After a series of heated conversations, a compromise had been reached. The lights were to be turned off at eleven p.m. each night. This was well after Holly's bedtime so they were always on while she was trying to get to sleep. She didn't ever complain to her father, though. She loved the lights as much as he did and felt that missing a few hours' sleep was a small price to pay.

Tonight, Holly stared at the ceiling as the Christmas lights pulsed through her curtains. She was thinking about Santa and his reindeer flying through the air, bringing (she hoped) a present for her.

CHAPTER THREE

Dave was exhausted. He had finally managed to stop talking and, like the other reindeer, concentrated now on galloping as fast as he could. This being his first Christmas, he was determined not to let the others down.

All the excitement of his first day on the job and all the nervous energy had drained away. So much so that Dave was feeling a little sleepy. Pulling the sleigh was tough work, and they had a long way to go before they could rest.

Dave had no idea where they were. Towns, cities and long stretches of water flashed by as they criss-crossed the globe. Soon all he was aware of was his own breathing and the breathing of the others. They veered left, then right, then left again. He drove himself on. Left again, right again. They swooped down across a stretch of houses, then banked sharply to the right and over a huge castle. Dropping down again across fields and meadows, they flashed over a wood with one small cottage in the middle of it.

Must be a child in that cottage, thought Dave, as his eyelids grew heavier and heavier. His head dropped forward as he nearly fell asleep, and then jerked upright as he realized what was happening.

You can't fall asleep! he scolded himself.

Come on!

He tried to concentrate on Rudolph in front of him. What would their leader say if Dave fell asleep on his first night on the job? But after a few moments he started to drift off again; his eyes felt heavy…

It was then that Rudolph farted. A thunderous, echoing, booming fart that startled Dave awake. Dave shouted, **"I'm awake!"** and flung his head back violently.

A couple of things flashed through his mind. The first was that Rudolph's fart really didn't smell like perfume. At least no perfume Dave had ever sniffed or wanted to sniff ever again. And secondly that his nose, as he had flung back his head, had come into contact with something solid.

In fact, his nose had clipped the pin holding

Rudolph's harness in place, flicking it out of its slot and sending it arcing high into the night air. It fell to the ground behind them.

Rudolph was now no longer connected to the rest of the reindeer and the sleigh, and he quickly began to pull ahead, completely unaware of what had happened. Rudolph noticed that he was suddenly flying faster, but put it down to his talent.

"I KNEW I WAS AMAZING ALREADY, BUT I'M SUDDENLY EVEN MORE AMAZING THAN I THOUGHT!" Rudolph shouted. Dave watched in horror.

Comet, the reindeer to Dave's right, who had been running with his head down, looked up and saw Rudolph tearing off without them and his mouth dropped open.

"What's happened?!"

"I..." began Dave, not really sure what to say. "I... He farted..."

"He *farted*?" said Comet. "And that turbocharged him?"

"No, he startled me and I might have accidentally ... disconnected him."

"You *might* have?"

"I *did*. I did disconnect him. That's what happened. I can't lie," admitted Dave, hoping that telling the truth would help.

Comet turned his head and made an extraordinary barking sound – a sound Dave had never heard a reindeer make before.

Santa appeared on the sleigh. He took in the situation in one glance, grabbed the reins and pulled hard. The reindeer began to slow and then headed straight down, slamming on to the roof of the first house they came to.

It was a small house in a cul-de-sac, a house lit up with thousands of lights. There were strings of lights along the line of the roof. Lights around every window. Lights around every door. Lights wrapped around the chimney. There were twelve illuminated Santas climbing up the walls. In the small front garden, there was an illuminated Nativity scene, fifteen illuminated reindeer, lots of snowmen, elves, Christmas trees and one big sleigh.

The real Santa sleigh skidded to a halt at an angle on the pitched roof. Dave nearly slid right off. He scrambled back from the edge, hoping he hadn't looked too silly.

There was a moment's silence.

Then Santa clicked his fingers and every light on the house and in the garden went out.

CHAPTER
FOUR

Holly was still awake when the lights went out. She had no idea what time it was, so figured it must be eleven p.m. It wasn't.

Her dad, Simon, had been in the living room listening to his favourite playlist – *101 Unusual Christmas Hits* – with his headphones in. Halfway through the song "Grandma Fell on an Elf", the lights went out. Simon assumed that the circuit had tripped.

He walked over to the cupboard that contained the circuit breaker and was surprised to see that there wasn't a problem. According to the circuit board, everything should be working properly.

Simon scratched his head. It couldn't be a power cut as the lights inside the house were working. But the Christmas lights outside weren't working. It didn't make any sense.

He decided to head into the loft. He walked up the stairs and grabbed the pole to open the loft hatch. It swung down and Simon hooked the extending ladder with the pole. He was trying to be as quiet as possible in order not to wake Holly.

But the moment Holly heard him, she leapt out of bed, put on her dressing gown and opened her door.

"Dad, what are you doing?"

"Holly! Go back to bed."

"I thought it was Santa."

"Do I look like Santa?"

"What are you doing?"

"The outside lights have gone out and I'm trying to find out why."

"Can I help?"

"Actually, you probably could. Put your

slippers on."

Holly did so, glad to be doing something other than lying in bed unable to sleep.

She followed her dad up the ladder and into the cramped loft. She hadn't been up there for years. There were cardboard boxes everywhere full of old toys, clothes and letters.

Also – The Trunk. The Trunk was a large trunk that Holly was absolutely forbidden to go anywhere near. Or even to talk about. She knew it contained her mum's letters and some other personal things that her dad had wanted to keep. But opening it wasn't allowed. Even talking about it was discouraged. Her dad had never got over losing his wife, and sometimes even mentioning her name made him more upset than he could handle. So The Trunk sat there and both Holly and her dad pretended to each other that it didn't exist.

"Grab that torch, would you, Hols?" he asked, unscrewing the plastic cover of a large unit fixed to the wall. **"Shine it over here so I can see what I'm doing."**

Simon often tried to get Holly interested in how electricity worked. He liked to explain all about circuits and transformers and amps and watts and volts, but Holly could never make sense of it. She didn't share her dad's enthusiasm for the subject. It was all gobbledygook to her.

"This is an extra service panel I put in to provide further protection," he said. **"The lights are a continuous load, so we need to make sure the amperage is within eight per cent of the max."**

Holly understood precisely none of this. Her

dad might as well have said, "**Biscuit flaps tickle brown sack juice in bouncy castle cheese.**" That would have made as much sense to her.

But Holly nodded. If she said she didn't understand then her dad would explain it all again, and she didn't want that.

Her dad inspected whatever it was he was inspecting, and then shook his head.

"**Doesn't make any sense,**" he said. "**Doesn't make any sense at all.**"

CHAPTER
FIVE

Dave could feel the other reindeer staring at him, but he didn't want to meet their eyes. He was so embarrassed. His first time pulling the sleigh and he'd been responsible for losing Rudolph.

Santa stood in front of his magic box. He looked cross. Any disruption to the schedule on this most important of nights bothered him. He took great pride in delivering presents to each and every child on his list.

He had to act quickly. Every second they were parked on the roof of this house increased their chance of discovery. This house, with all its Santas and reindeer and decorations, was the perfect place to blend in and hide, but he didn't want to push his luck.

The magic box not only allowed Santa to slow down time but also contained the coordinates of every house they needed to deliver presents to and the exact position of Santa, the sleigh and all the individual reindeer. In other words, the magic box could tell Santa where Rudolph was. Then they could go and fetch him back.

Opening the lid, Santa felt the air around the box crackle and snap. The box contained magic of extraordinary power and needed to be handled carefully.

A screen under the lid flickered into life and the word USERNAME appeared. Santa typed in SANTA1 and pressed ENTER. The next screen said PASSWORD.

Santa scratched his head. He could never remember his password.

"Dasher?" he called out. "What's my password again?"

Dasher sighed. Santa had the worst memory. "Your username is SANTA1, no gaps, all capitals. Your password is XMAS UNDERSCORE BIG UNDERSCORE BOY."

"That's right," said Santa. "I remember now."

He typed in the password and a new page appeared saying, "Our system thinks you might be a robot! Please click on all the bicycles in the image below."

Santa hated doing this. Why would anyone think he was a robot? He was Santa! He clicked on all the images he thought had bicycles in but must have got it wrong because another page appeared: **"Click on all the fire hydrants."**

This annoyed him because they didn't have fire hydrants at the North Pole. They were, he thought, an American thing, and he didn't have time to check out fire hydrants when they were whooshing through the United States.

Eventually, after having to click on all the traffic lights, then all the motorbikes, then all the bridges, then all the cars, then all the ham sandwiches, then all the chicken feet, he must have finally clicked all the

right squares because the system let him through. Only to find a page saying that a new software update was being installed and could he please wait.

Santa let out a growl of frustration; Dave hung his head even lower as snow started to fall.

CHAPTER SIX

"Let's go and check out the connections on the roof," Holly's dad said. "Maybe that's where the issue is."

"Are you sure that's a good idea?" Holly said. "It's started snowing."

"You hold the ladder and I'll climb up," said Simon, ignoring her.

They put on coats, hats, scarves and gloves and headed outside. It was bitterly cold and the snow was falling heavily now.

"Dad," said Holly as Simon took the long ladder from the garage and placed it against the roof, "please be careful up there! It'll be slippery."

"Right, stand on the bottom rung to keep it stable," he said, "and I'll climb up."

And without another word, up he climbed. Inspecting the cables, everything looked good. He wanted to check the junction box by the chimney, so he climbed right to the top.

Again, the junction box looked fine, but when he peered over to the far side of the roof, Holly's dad was confronted by an extraordinary sight: eight real reindeer with clouds of steam coming off them, a huge sleigh and Santa Claus staring at a screen set into the top of a big glowing red box.

Holly's dad's mouth fell open and he let out a gasp of astonishment. He stood bolt upright. He tried to speak but couldn't. He could feel his heart thumping in his throat.

He found himself croaking, **"Hello, Santa. My name's Simon. I love you."**

The eight reindeer looked up. Santa looked up. For a moment, they all stared at each other.

Then Holly's dad realized he was falling backwards. He tried to grab the ladder, but his flailing arms couldn't get a grip on it.

Thrashing about wildly, his right hand managed to grasp one of the electric cables tied to the chimney and he hung on to it for dear life. As he fell, the cable ties holding the cable in place snapped one by one, until he slid backwards and upside down off the roof towards a terrified Holly.

At that moment Santa's screen flashed up: **UPDATE COMPLETE.** *Thank you for your patience. Would you like to complete a short customer survey before you go?* The magic box turned from red to green. Just as …

… the electric cable that Holly's dad was holding snapped. There was a massive explosion, a blinding white light, the smell of burning hair and a shower of multi-coloured sparks.

Holly closed her eyes and covered her head and face with her arms, bracing herself for the worst. She stood like that for some time, wondering if her father had landed on her and she'd died and gone to heaven. When eventually she dared look, there was no sign of her dad.

46

Instead, standing next to her, was a reindeer with a sheepish grin on his face.

"Hello," said the reindeer. "My name's Dave. We have a problem."

CHAPTER SEVEN

"You're telling me that you're one of the reindeer that pulls Santa's sleigh?" asked an astonished Holly.

"That's right," said Dave, as gently and as calmly as he could.

"The actual real Santa?"

"The actual real Santa, yes."

"The actual real-life Santa from the North Pole who flies around and delivers presents and says, 'Ho! Ho! Ho!'?"

"Yes, the actual real-life Santa from the North Pole who flies around and delivers presents. But I've never heard him say, 'Ho! Ho! Ho!' so I can't be sure about that bit."

"And he was on *our roof*?"

"Correct."

"But he's gone now?"

"Yup."

"And you don't know where he went?"

"No. There was an explosion. Santa vanished and so did all the other reindeer. Except Rudolph – he'd flown off already. And I ended up down here."

"And my dad's gone too?"

"Looks like it."

"And you don't know where *he* is either?"

"Sorry, no."

"And you're Blitzen, but you're the new

Blitzen not the old Blitzen? Your real name is ... Dave?"

"Yes."

Holly looked down at the ground, trying to take all this in. She had loved Christmas ever since she was a little girl. Meeting one of the actual reindeer that pulled Santa's sleigh should have been like meeting a superstar. She just hadn't expected it to happen like *this*. Or for the reindeer to be called Dave. Or for him to be able to talk. She wasn't sure what to say, so she said, **"This is all pretty weird."**

"I know," said Dave. He was trying to give Holly time to get her head around the situation, but it wasn't easy to be patient. He felt sick with worry and knew they needed to move quickly.

"So Santa's sleigh is still up there?" said Holly.

"Yes."

"**Show me,**" said Holly, adding, "**please.**" She didn't want to appear rude.

Dave looked at the ladder.

"**I'm not very good with ladders,**" said Dave, "**on account of me being a reindeer and having hooves and everything. You can go up, though.**"

"**I'm not allowed on the roof.**"

"**Oh.**"

"**Perhaps I should go round to the front of the house and look?**"

"**That should work.**"

Holly led Dave through the side gate and into the front garden, thinking all the while *I'm having a conversation with a talking reindeer. A real-life reindeer. Dad would love this! I can't believe he's missing it.*

Dave scampered behind a bush.

"What are you doing?" asked Holly.

"Don't want anyone to see me," hissed Dave. "Santa would be furious if I were spotted."

"Oh."

Holly looked up at the roof. The snow was falling heavily now. Sure enough, there was a large sleigh parked up there, next to a glowing green box.

"I see it," she said. "Now what?" She thought for a moment. "Maybe they got blasted through the roof and are inside the house. I'm going in to look."

"Can I come?" asked Dave nervously. "I don't want to be out here on my own."

Holly thought for a moment. Normally she wouldn't even consider inviting a stranger into her house, but these were rather extraordinary circumstances. She nodded and walked around the house to the back garden. Dave followed her, darting from shadow to shadow.

Inside the back door, Holly took off her wellies.

"Please wipe your feet, Dave. Sorry, your paws. I mean hooves!" she said. **"I've never had a reindeer over before, sorry."**

"No probs," said Dave, wiping his hooves on the mat.

He was a big reindeer with large antlers. He could only just squeeze into the narrow hallway.

"Let's look in the kitchen first," said Holly. She headed into the kitchen. Dave followed, his antlers scraping the walls on either side, knocking off three framed pictures of Holly's mum that Holly had painted when she was little.

"Sorry!" said Dave.

He tilted his head and rather awkwardly edged down the corridor and through into the kitchen.

"Maybe you wait here," suggested Holly as Dave clumsily bashed a small side table knocking everything on it to the floor, "and I'll have a look around for them."

"Good plan."

"Don't want you breaking everything in the house."

"Got it. And, Holly..."

"Yes?"

"I don't want to be pushy, but please could you hurry? We haven't got much time."

"We?" replied Holly. "What's with the 'we'?"

"I was rather hoping you'd help me save Christmas."

"Save Christmas?"

"Yes," said Dave. "There won't be a Christmas if we don't find Santa and the other reindeer."

"Won't there?"

"No."

Holly gulped. She started to feel a bit sick. Christmas was important. It was important to children all over the world. But it was really, really important to her and Dad.

"In that case, I'll be as quick as I can."

CHAPTER EIGHT

Not long after, Holly and Dave were back in the front garden looking up at the sleigh again. Holly had found nobody in the house. No Santa, no Dad and no reindeer.

"What next?" she asked.

"You see the glowing green box?" whispered Dave.

Holly nodded.

"That's Santa's magic box. It's the thing that helps us to fly. It should also be able to tell us

where everyone is."

"It *should?*" said Holly suspiciously. "Don't you *know* what the magic box does?"

"Not really. This is only my first day in the job."

"Your first day!" Holly exclaimed. "Oh wow! This gets better and better."

"Oh good!" said Dave, not understanding Holly's sarcasm.

"No, not good. When I said better and better, I meant worse and worse."

"Then why did you say...?"

"Forget it! How do we get that box? I can't go on to the roof and you can't climb the ladder."

"I can fly."

Holly stared at Dave. Despite all her worries about her dad, she felt a flash of excitement.

"Really? You can actually fly? That's not just made up?"

"Really. We can fly. That's how we pull the sleigh through the air. I'll fly up there and bring the sleigh and the magic box down."

"Good plan," said Holly. "Go on then!"

Dave hesitated. He did not want to admit to Holly that he had never flown on his own before. Earlier, Santa had hooked all the reindeer up to the sleigh in the snow by the North Pole and they had run and taken off almost immediately. He hadn't really known how it had happened, just that it had. He'd been flying all night, so surely he could do it again now. Couldn't he?

Dave took a deep breath and bolted down the small garden. He was young and strong and fast and was travelling at great speed in no time. He looked up and willed his body to take to the air. Despite hours of flying he felt good, he felt elated, he felt confident, he—

Crashed straight into the fence at the end of the garden.

Holly ran over to him. **"Are you all right?"**

"OW!" Dave shouted. **"That really hurt!"**

"What happened? Why didn't you fly?"

Dave thought about it. **"Maybe I didn't have enough space."**

"Then you'll have to go to the road out front."

"But someone might see me—"

"Simon?" called out a voice. **"Is that you? I heard a terrible crash..."**

Mrs Dithers from next door! Holly put her finger to her lips. Mrs Dithers was the last person on Earth that Holly wanted to see right now.

"Why have you turned off your Christmas lights?" called out Mrs Dithers in her thin voice. **"What's happening?"**

Mrs Dithers was a nosy parker, always and relentlessly into everybody else's business. As far as Holly could tell, she just spent all her days sat looking out of her front window. Holly couldn't remember ever not seeing her there. When Holly left for school in the morning: Mrs Dithers watched her go. When Holly came back from school: Mrs Dithers was there. She was always there, the sunshine glinting off her small round glasses. Whenever Holly went anywhere, whatever time of day or night: Mrs Dithers was there looking out her front window.

"Doesn't she have a TV?" Holly had once said to her dad. **"Or a book? Or ever need to eat or go to the toilet?"**

Mrs Dithers also always seemed to be wearing the same outfit: a frilly white lace dress. Rumour was she had worn it in a school play when she was a teenager and had never taken it off. Nobody knew if that was really true, but everyone agreed that the dress must smell pretty bad by now.

The only thing that ever changed about Mrs Dithers was her hair. She seemed to have a huge collection of wigs. One day she would be sporting a black bob, the next a huge mass of curly blonde ringlets, the next a red perm. No two days were the same.

Dave scrambled to his feet and, again,

Holly signalled that he needed to be quiet. The two of them stood silently as the snow fell, clouds of condensation coming out of both their mouths.

"Simon?" came Mrs Dithers' voice again. Then, after an agonizing few moments, Holly and Dave heard her back door closing again.

Holly breathed a sigh of relief and whispered, **"Let's try and get you out the front, Dave, so that you can try taking off on the road. We'll just have to be careful not to be seen by Mrs Dithers."**

They walked back up the garden to Holly's back door. The snow may have been falling heavily, but at least it helped to muffle the sound of Dave's hooves on the patio.

Holly opened the back door, turned to let Dave inside and stopped still.

There, standing on the other side of the fence, wearing her tatty white lacy dress under a pink beehive, stood Mrs Dithers, staring at Dave, her mouth open in total astonishment.

Holly and Dave didn't hang about. They bolted in the back door, through the house, Dave taking all remaining pictures and half  the wallpaper off the wall with his antlers as he did so, and out the front door as fast as they could. They'd have to deal with the fallout

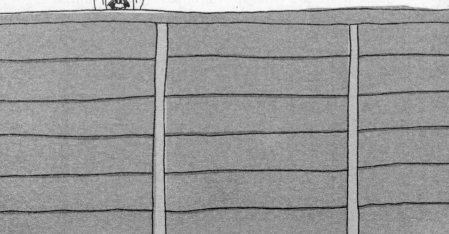

from Dave being spotted by Mrs Dithers later. For now, the most important thing was to get on to the roof and to the magic box.

As they tore down the front path, Holly looked over her shoulder and was astonished to see Mrs Dithers already sat looking out of her front window, her hair now a brunette French plait.

Dave leapt over the garden gate with ease and Holly, too small to do the same, flung open the gate and ran after him.

"Go!" she hissed. **"Try to fly! Go! I'll wait here!"**

She slowed and watched as Dave galloped off down the road. Holly hoped the snow, almost a blizzard at this stage, would hide Dave from the neighbours' view.

Soon, he was out of sight and Holly looked

around her at the silent street, the snow stinging her eyes, in her dressing gown and slippers, suddenly freezing and slightly frightened. Was this really happening? Was she really standing in the cold, late on Christmas Eve, waiting to see if a reindeer could fly? Where had her dad gone? And was it really up to her and Dave to save Christmas for the whole world?

She started to tremble and bit her bottom lip in an effort not to start crying. She needed to be strong, she told herself; she needed to think clearly. This was no time to crumble. She hoped Dave would come back soon. Things seemed much bleaker now she was on her own.

Then, far off, in the direction that Dave had headed, came the sounds of an enormous crash and a car alarm going off. She strained to see through the snow, but it was falling harder than ever. She looked up, half hoping to see Dave swoop above her, but there was nothing except a frenzy of snowflakes.

Without warning, Dave reappeared, tearing past her, very much *not* flying.

"Quick!" he shouted as he hurtled past. He veered left up Holly's small driveway and she started after him. Running as fast as she could, almost losing her footing in the ever-deepening snow, she burst through the open front door, slamming it shut behind her. She skidded to a halt beside Dave, who was gasping for air after his exertions and there, before them in the narrow hallway, both wearing tatty white lacy dresses, one with a pink beehive and one with a brunette French plait, stood not one but *two* Mrs Ditherses.

Dave burst into tears and then so did Holly.

CHAPTER NINE

Holly sat at the kitchen table and cradled the mug of hot chocolate made for her by Mrs Dithers (the one with the pink beehive). Dave slurped his noisily from a bowl. Mrs Dithers and Mrs Dithers had taken one look at the cold, shivering, crying pair and decided that hot chocolate was the answer.

Dave had taken quite a while to calm down. When the tears had come, he couldn't stop them. He kept wailing, "**My first day and I've** lost Santa and his reindeer!" and, "If only you hadn't farted, Rudolph!"

Holly, too, wept for some time. "My dad's disappeared!" she cried. She was also pretty freaked out to be sitting in her kitchen with a talking reindeer called Dave and two identical (apart from the hair) Mrs Ditherses, but she didn't say anything about that.

The twin Mrs Ditherses said nothing; they quickly made the hot chocolates and found two blankets for Holly and Dave, then sat side by side at the table and waited for Holly and Dave to regain their composure.

Holly took another sip of hot chocolate, sighed heavily, wiped her eyes and looked up. Mrs Dithers and Mrs Dithers looked back at her. They really were identical. Pale, almost ghostly white skin, a wart on the left side of each chin, identical high-necked white lacy long-sleeved dresses, no jewellery, heavily made-up eyes, yellowing teeth, long immaculate fingernails at the end of thin, bony, veiny fingers. And they were short. Holly was only twelve, but she was already much taller than either of them. They looked like two slightly frayed aging porcelain dolls.

"Sorry," said Holly. "It was quite a shock seeing you in our hallway. Especially as I didn't know there were two of you."

The Mrs Dithers with the French plait nodded gently.

"I suppose I should explain," Holly went on. Then she looked at Dave. "Actually, you'll have to explain, Dave, because I can't."

Dave cleared his throat. "First of all, sorry about all the crying and the stuff about

Rudolph farting. It's been a very stressful time."

One Mrs Dithers nodded, but the other Mrs Dithers didn't.

"It's a long story, but we need to get on to Holly's roof," Dave continued. "We have to get the magic box from the roof or…" Here he started to choke up again. "Or we won't find Santa or the reindeer or Holly's dad and Christmas might not happen. And I think it'll all be my fault."

"I'm not allowed on the roof," said Holly. "I promised my dad and I can't break my promise. Plus, it's snowing really heavily. It's dangerous."

"And I can't fly, it seems," said Dave, "without the magic box."

Mrs Dithers looked at the other Mrs

Dithers, and, without saying a word, they got up and walked out of the back door. Holly ran to follow them, Dave close behind.

Outside, the snow was still falling heavily and the garden was grey-white in the moonlight. Holly could still hear the car alarm in the distance.

"Is that alarm anything to do with you?" Holly asked Dave.

"A car appeared out of nowhere as I was running down the road and I ... jumped over it. I think I gave the driver a shock because she drove into a parked car."

"Oh, you would have shocked the driver all right. Was she hurt?"

"No, I don't think so. She was making a call when I came back."

Holly looked for the Mrs Ditherses, but

they were nowhere to be seen in the blinding blizzard. Holly was about to call out when they appeared out of the whiteness, two white figures, carrying a ladder. Holly and Dave jumped out of the way to let them pass and turned to follow.

Round the front of the house, the two old ladies wasted no time in extending the ladder and propping it up against the side of the house. The beehived Mrs Dithers began to climb while the French-plaited Mrs Dithers stood at the bottom of the ladder, keeping it steady.

Once at the top, beehive Mrs Dithers reached for the glowing box, the only thing emitting any light on the roof that normally winked and shone with red, yellow, green, white and blue lights. The box was about the size of a cool box and had a crown of snow on it the depth of a book. It was just out of her reach. Mrs Dithers strained to get a finger on it but came up short. She stood on tiptoes. It helped a bit but not enough.

Surely she won't climb on to the roof, thought Holly. *It will be so slippery with all this snow.*

Panting, beehive Mrs Dithers thought for a moment. She turned to look down at the other Mrs Dithers. They said nothing, but Holly knew they were engaged in some kind of silent conversation with each other. After a few moments, beehive Mrs Dithers nodded gently, reached up and pulled off her wig. Underneath she was almost completely bald, save a few wispy strands of white hair at the front and back of her head.

Swinging the beehive wig wildly at the magic box, she connected at the second

attempt. The box began to slide slowly down the roof. Holly instinctively took a step towards it to try and catch it when it fell. It wasn't very big, but she had no idea how heavy it was.

"**Leave it**," whispered Dave. "**It'll be fine. Let it fall.**"

Holly took a step back again as the box slid off the edge of the roof and watched as it floated gently down to the ground like it weighed no more than a feather.

Holly found it hard to take her eyes off it. It throbbed gently, pulsing with a lime green light and emitted a low hum.

"**Open the lid, Holly,**" instructed Dave.

Holly did so as beehive Mrs Dithers, her wig now back in place, and French plait Mrs Dithers joined them.

Inside the box, a screen flickered to life.

The word USERNAME appeared.

"SANTA1," said Dave. "I heard Santa talking about this earlier."

Holly typed it in and pressed ENTER. The screen said PASSWORD.

"XMAS UNDERSCORE BIG UNDERSCORE BOY," said Dave, and Holly typed.

"Thank goodness you're here," said Dave. "Typing would be a nightmare with these hooves."

On the screen:

WELCOME BACK,
SANTA1

After a few seconds it faded and this appeared:

**THOUGHT FOR THE DAY: -
ALWAYS GIVE 100%
UNLESS YOU ARE
DONATING BLOOD!**

Dave, Holly and the Mrs Ditherses watched as the screen faded to black again. One by one the following lines appeared for a few seconds before fading away:

**24TH DECEMBER
TODAY'S TO-DO LIST:
BUY CAT LITTER
DELIVER PRESENTS TO ALL THE
CHILDREN IN THE WORLD
CLEAN FRIDGE**

TODAY'S INTERESTING FACT:
IN LEONARDO DA VINCI'S
PAINTING, THE MONA LISA
HAS NO EYEBROWS

ON THIS DAY:
"SILENT NIGHT" WAS
FIRST PERFORMED IN
1818 IN AUSTRIA

MENU
(Please select one of the below)
FLIGHT MODE
PRESENT COLLECTION
PRESENT DELIVERY
TIME
TRACKING
HOME
CLEAN
EMERGENCY TOILET

80

This last list stayed on the screen.

"Wow!" said Holly. "That's amazing!"

"I know!" exclaimed Dave. "I never knew Santa had a cat!"

"No, I meant the magic box is amazing."

"Oh, right," said Dave. "Yes, I suppose it is. So we need to press TRACKING to find out where everyone went, then I'll try and fly up to get the sleigh down. I should be able to fly now I'm with the magic box. I certainly hope so. Then we can go and get everyone."

"*We?*" exclaimed Holly, both excited and scared by the idea. "I have to go with you? In the sleigh?"

Dave looked at her with his big reindeer eyes. "Please," he said quietly. "I don't want to have to do this on my own."

"But you're a reindeer. One of Santa's

reindeer – this is what you do. Fly around with the sleigh. I'm a girl who should be in bed. It's *way* past my bedtime."

"I know but…" Dave faltered, and Holly thought he might start crying again. "I'll get scared on my own. Please."

Holly looked up at the huge sleigh parked on their roof. Part of her couldn't think of anything more thrilling than flying in Santa's sleigh; it was literally something she had dreamed about, but it felt a bit overwhelming too.

"Won't I get cold?"

"It's heated."

"Is it dangerous?"

"Not really."

"*Not really?* I wanted to hear 'no, not dangerous at all'. *Not really* is worrying because it means it's a little bit dangerous."

"Look," said Dave, "I know this whole thing is my fault, but it'll be quicker if we do it together. I can't type things into the magic box without you."

"And the magic box will take us to Santa and the reindeer and my dad?"

"Well, sort of," said Dave. He wasn't meeting Holly's eye.

"Why only *sort of*?" said Holly.

"Well, your dad isn't fitted with a tracker, you see. So the magic box might not be able to find him." Holly stared open-mouthed at Dave, too shocked to speak. "But I'm sure they'll all be together," Dave hurried on. "They're probably just round the corner somewhere!"

Dave tried to arrange his face so that it looked hopeful and sincere and kind to reassure Holly.

Holly said, **"What are you doing? Do you need to go to the toilet?"**

"I'm trying to look hopeful and sincere and kind."

"Well, you look like you're trying to do a poo," said Holly, suddenly feeling cross and upset. **"Stop it."**

She had liked this reindeer when they had first met, but now she just wanted her dad back.

Dave bit his bottom lip to stop it trembling. He felt wracked with guilt. Guilt for unhooking Rudolph and causing this whole kerfuffle, and guilt for trying to involve this girl in the rescue, but what choice did he have?

"OK," said Holly. **"Let's try and find them."**

"Great!" said Dave, more cheerfully than he felt. **"Please press TRACKING on the screen."**

Holly did so. A further menu appeared:

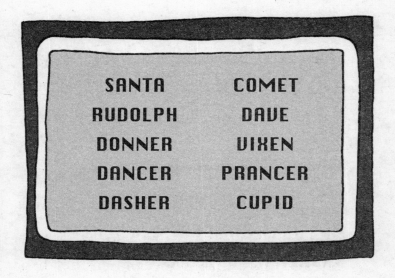

```
SANTA        COMET
RUDOLPH      DAVE
DONNER       VIXEN
DANCER       PRANCER
DASHER       CUPID
```

"You were right," Holly said. "There's no sign of my dad."

"We'll find him," said Dave. "Let's get Santa first; he'll know what to do."

Holly pressed **SANTA**.

Nothing happened.

She pressed it again.

Nothing.

She looked at Dave. He shrugged. Or tried to – shrugging doesn't come naturally to reindeer.

"What now?" she asked.

"Let's try Rudolph. He's a bit annoying, but he is *Rudolph* so he should be able to work this out."

Holly pressed **RUDOLPH**. Nothing happened.

Holly pressed **DONNER**. Nothing happened.

She pressed **DANCER**. Nothing happened.

DASHER was no better.

With a sigh, she pressed **COMET**. Nothing.

When she pressed **DAVE**, the box turned from green to yellow and they heard a small metallic *ding* noise. On the screen appeared a spinning picture of the Earth. Holly recognized the United States of America as it spun past, then the huge expanse of the Pacific Ocean, across Asia and Europe. When Great Britain appeared, the image stopped spinning and zoomed in until it came to a halt over a picture of Holly's house. A red light flashed and next to it the word **DAVE**.

Holly looked up. **"We know where you are then, Dave,"** she said flatly. **"You're here."**

"At least it works!" said Dave, trying to sound optimistic.

Holly tried **VIXEN**, nothing. **PRANCER**, nothing.

The last one was **CUPID**.

"Should I even bother?" she said. **"Or shall we leave this a mystery and go inside, and hope I wake up tomorrow and discover that this has all been a bad dream?"**

"I think the curiosity would kill me," said Dave, **"but it doesn't look good, does it?"**

Holly stabbed at the last name. Nothing happened.

At first.

Then the screen went blank.

The box turned yellow. The spinning image of the Earth appeared on the screen: the Pacific Ocean, Asia, Europe all flashed by. As it moved across the Atlantic, the spinning image began to slow and then, as before, zoomed in revealing Cupid's location.

Holly, stunned, turned to Dave. **"Cupid's in New York! And, by the looks of it, she's on top of the Empire State Building!"**

CHAPTER TEN

They were going to New York. But first, Holly needed to get dressed.

She rushed into the house and put on as many layers as she could. She didn't entirely trust Dave's claim that the sleigh was heated. The malfunctioning magic box hadn't given her much confidence in the whole operation.

Rushing downstairs, she found Mrs Dithers and Mrs Dithers in the kitchen.

"Will you please stay here in case Dad turns

up?" she asked them. "If he comes back and I'm not here, he'll worry. You can tell him where I am."

Mrs Dithers and Mrs Dithers just blinked at her.

"I'll take that as a yes. Thanks!" said Holly and ran back outside to where Dave was waiting.

"What's the plan?" asked Holly.

"Log in again and put us in FLIGHT MODE. Now we've got the magic box I can fly on to the roof and push the sleigh off."

"You can't drop a massive sleigh like that!" said Holly. "You'll break it."

"Don't worry," replied Dave. "It'll float down just like the magic box."

"Why don't you fly it down?"

"I can't fit myself to the harness. I can't tell you how annoying it is not having hands. I'd give anything to have fingers and thumbs like you, rather than these big old hooves."

Holly flicked open the magic box, typed in **SANTA1** and the password **XMAS_BIG_ BOY**, and then pressed **FLIGHT MODE**. The box changed from green to purple and Dave shuddered as it did so.

"Ooh, I remember that feeling," he said. **"When I felt it before I thought I was just excited to be working for Santa, but it must have been us being put into flight mode. I should be able to fly now."**

He started forward and within a step or two, he was airborne.

"Woohoo!" said Holly. Things were looking up.

Dave swooped out over the road gaining height, then doubled back, landing silently on the snow-covered roof. He walked over to the other side of the sleigh, lowered his head and tried to push it off the roof.

It resisted at first, then all at once it began to move. It slid slowly down the roof, pushing snow ahead of it, chunks plopping on to the garden path.

Dave shoved with all his might. The sleigh gathered pace, reached the edge of the roof and fell off it, plummeting like a stone, landing on its side on the path below with an almighty crack.

Holly put one hand to her mouth in shock and the other on to the magic box, instinctively, to protect it.

She watched, horrified, as Dave, moving with too much momentum to stop, fell off the roof too, straight into the bush next to the front door.

He rolled over and stood up. Holly ran over to him.

"I'm fine, I'm fine," he said. "That didn't go to plan."

They inspected the sleigh. There was a big crack along one side.

"Santa's going to be furious," Dave said. "He loves this sleigh."

"Why did you think it would float down?"

"I just thought it would. Magic, you know. I'm making a mess of this already, aren't I?" said Dave glumly.

"You're doing your best," said Holly, trying to reassure him. "That's all you can do."

"Yes, I suppose so," said Dave with a shy smile. "Come on, let's get going. Hook me up."

It took them several minutes to work out how all the straps and buckles worked. There were a lot of them – enough for nine reindeer – so they had to figure out which ones they needed and which ones they didn't. There was a mass of leather straps, all muddled up like a bowl of spaghetti.

When, finally, Dave was strapped in, Holly lifted the magic box on to the sleigh and put it on a plinth which had a brass plaque with **MAGIC BOX** written on it.

At the front of the sleigh was a large and comfortable leather armchair that Holly slid into. It was so big her feet didn't touch the floor, so she crossed her legs hoping Santa wouldn't mind her shoes touching his chair. Her dad hated her wearing her shoes indoors at all, let alone plonking them on the furniture. He insisted they both took their shoes off by the front door, which was fine but her dad always had holes in his socks and wandered around with his hairy toes poking out the end.

Behind Santa's armchair, the floor of the sleigh was empty. There were several brass handles fitted into it and Holly assumed that they opened compartments to where the presents for the children were stored. She was tempted to have a look; her own present was probably in there somewhere. She'd asked Santa for a pony this year but didn't have much hope of getting one. And it didn't look like there would be room for a pony under there anyway. In fact, how could Santa store enough presents down there for all the deliveries he had to make?

"Are we still in FLIGHT MODE?" Dave shouted.

Holly checked. "Yes!"

"Then hold on!"

Holly gripped the arms of the chair tightly as Dave surged forward and up, leaping high into the air on his third stride. The straps attaching him to the sleigh tightened, Holly prepared for flight, but the sleigh didn't budge an inch.

Dave galloped as hard as he could, but he wasn't moving forwards at all, just running on the spot. He strained with huge exertion, redoubling his efforts, bobbing about like a helium balloon attached to a post. The sleigh went nowhere.

Dave did not give up, running so hard his eyes started to bulge and his tongue flopped out the side of his mouth. After nearly a minute of this, Dave gave up and dropped down to the roof. He was a fit young reindeer, but he was gasping for breath.

"What's wrong?" asked Holly.

Dave wasn't able to talk yet; he gulped down huge lungfuls of air.

"Too heavy?" asked Holly. **"I suppose there's a reason why there are normally nine of you."**

Dave rolled over in the snow to try to cool himself down, still panting heavily.

"Maybe we should leave some of the presents here? To lighten your load?"

Dave tried to speak but still couldn't.

"I'll have a look in the hold," she said. **"I presume it's called the hold? That's what you'd call it in a ship, I think. Anyway, let's have a look."**

Holly climbed out of Santa's armchair and walked to the back of the sleigh. There were several handles to choose from. She picked one at random. It was unlocked; she lifted it and a square lid swung open, revealing a ladder heading down into the darkness below.

"Is there a light?" asked Holly.

"Don't know." Dave had finally recovered enough to talk. "We're not allowed in there. Just Santa."

"Well, I guess these are extraordinary circumstances," said Holly and started to climb backwards down the ladder. Dave couldn't believe how brave she was being.

As she climbed down, Holly peered into the gloom but couldn't see anything. Suddenly, lights flickered on and Holly was shocked by what she was looking at. A vast, cavernous space; the size, she guessed, of a football pitch and as high as a house. The space was full of rows and rows of shelves, containing thousands and thousands of presents, all beautifully and neatly wrapped, all with a name and address on the shelf in front of them. Some of the shelves were empty: presents already delivered, presumed Holly.

She stopped and stared. She felt a little dizzy. How was this possible? The sleigh was only the size of a minibus.

Climbing back up into the night air, it was her turn to take some big gulps of air.

"You all right?" asked Dave.

"I think so," said Holly. "There are *a lot* of presents down there."

"Sure," said Dave. "There are *a lot* of children in the world. So, what's the plan?"

"We're going to have to leave some presents here to make the sleigh lighter," said Holly. "But how?"

"Try the magic box," suggested Dave.

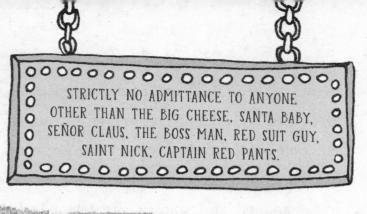

STRICTLY NO ADMITTANCE TO ANYONE
OTHER THAN THE BIG CHEESE, SANTA BABY,
SEÑOR CLAUS, THE BOSS MAN, RED SUIT GUY,
SAINT NICK, CAPTAIN RED PANTS.

Holly flicked open the box, typed in Santa's username and password, and considered her options.

FLIGHT MODE
PRESENT COLLECTION
PRESENT DELIVERY
TIME
TRACKING
HOME
CLEAN
EMERGENCY TOILET

"PRESENT DELIVERY?" she suggested. "Would that get rid of them?"

"We usually drop them off one by one," said Dave. "What we want is to get rid of them in one go. Perhaps try CLEAN?"

Holly pressed that option. A further screen appeared:

WASH AND WAX SLEIGH
REINDEER BATH AND SCRUB
SANTA SHOWER
SANTA BEARD STYLING
SANTA MANI–PEDI
RUDOLPH NOSE–REDDENING
CHAIR VACUUM
PRESENT CHAMBERS

Holly pressed **PRESENT CHAMBERS** and another screen appeared.

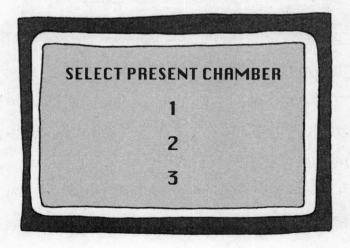

SELECT PRESENT CHAMBER
1
2
3

"There are *three* of them?" said Holly. "Are they all that big?"

"No idea," said Dave. "Just pick one."

Holly pressed 1.

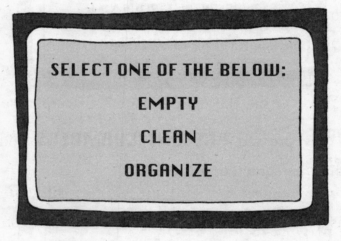

SELECT ONE OF THE BELOW:

EMPTY

CLEAN

ORGANIZE

"Empty!" said Holly. "Shall I do it?"

"I guess so," said a nervous-looking Dave.

Holly and Dave looked at each other for a moment, and then Holly pressed the button.

Instantly, they were at the height of the top of the chimney, looking down on the countryside around them. The sleigh and Dave sat atop an enormous mound of presents that completely engulfed her house, filling Holly's front and back gardens, some spilling out on to the path in front of the house. Half of Mrs Ditherses' garden was full of presents too.

"What have we done?" Holly said, appalled. "You can see the train station from up here and it's miles away! Do you think my house will be OK?"

"What about Mrs Dithers and Mrs Dithers?" asked Dave, struggling to keep his balance on the huge pile of carefully wrapped presents.

"Presents are mostly packaging, aren't they? Perhaps they're not as heavy as they seem."

"Dunno," said Dave. "But we need to get on with rescuing Cupid. At least then we'll have another pair of hooves to help."

"All right," said Holly. "Let's go. Let's hope the sleigh is light enough now!"

She flicked the sleigh into **FLIGHT MODE** again and selected the **EMPIRE STATE BUILDING** as their destination.

"Here we go!" yelled Dave, leaping forward and up. This time the sleigh moved too. Holly was thrown backwards in the armchair as Dave began to climb vertically – and soon he and Holly and the sleigh were a speck in the distance.

CHAPTER ELEVEN

Holly had never felt a sensation like it. They shot into the sky like a bullet fired from a gun, accelerating so quickly that she was pinned to the back of the big armchair. Her head and body felt incredibly heavy.

As they streaked skywards, Holly felt her eyesight go blurry and the skin on her face ripple. The wind was extraordinary, the strongest she'd ever encountered and deafeningly loud, and yet she wasn't cold at all.

Dave was right, it seemed, about the heating in the sleigh.

They were moving so fast, she couldn't look back at where they'd come from and, given the swirling snow, it was hard making sense of what was in front.

They burst through the clouds and out into a beautiful clear star-filled sky. Holly would have gasped with the wonder of it if she'd been able to, but all she could do was stare at the twinkling canopy above. A million stars winked and blinked at her with startling intensity. There was the moon, so bright and so near she felt she could reach out and touch it.

How high up are we? she wondered. It felt as though they had left Earth's atmosphere and were in space. Was that possible?

Dave slowed and, for a second, Holly felt

completely weightless. It reminded her of the feeling you get when a roller coaster plummets and your stomach seems to flip upside down. She loved the sensation.

Dave turned to look at her and smiled. He gracefully changed direction, pointing back down. The whole Earth spread out below Holly: dark, magnificent and breathtakingly beautiful.

Dave began to gallop once more, Holly was slammed back into the chair and they plunged Earthwards.

Geography was one of her favourite subjects, but she couldn't work out where they were. Huge weather systems of cloud obscured much of what was below. She could see vast patches of sea and ocean and patches, too, of white snow-covered land.

Then, all at once, they burst through the clouds and there, laid out splendidly below them, a million streetlights twinkling in the darkness, was New York City. Holly recognized the shape of Manhattan, one of the most talked-about and exciting places on Earth.

They streaked through the night sky. Down and down. Dave, guided by the magic box, knew exactly where he was heading, straight to the Empire State Building, to where Cupid had been flung after the explosion at Holly's house.

Holly hoped they weren't too late.

The mass of twinkling streetlights soon separated out into distinct buildings and streets. And there it was, the Empire State Building. Dave swooped south to get a better angle to approach. There was a huge sharp steel spire at the top of the Empire State Building and the last thing Dave wanted was to impale himself on it.

Banking low over the Upper Bay, Dave started to slow down as they whipped past the Statue of Liberty. Holly thought for a second that the statue had winked at them as they passed, but that wasn't possible, surely? Past Ellis Island, famous as the gateway to America for millions of immigrants, across the water towards the skyscrapers of Wall Street, up Fifth Avenue, over the Flatiron Building and there it was again, the Empire State Building.

The magic box had told them that Cupid was at the top of it, so Dave headed towards the Observation Deck on the one hundred and second floor.

Holly was wondering why no one had spotted them, but Dave knew the answer to that. Santa had explained earlier that people's brains work quite slowly. If they get a good long look at something, then it'll register in their minds. But if something zips by in a flash, they tend not to notice it. Especially if it's something they've never seen before. Their brains can't process the information quickly enough. The sleigh flashes across their vision, out of the corner of their eye and they don't take it in. Or at least they try to explain it away as something else entirely. This was how Santa managed to fly through towns and cities unnoticed.

Dave circled the building at speed twice before he saw Cupid. She was indeed at the top of the Empire State Building – the very, very top, her harness hooked over the spire, her legs dangling below.

She seemed to notice the sleigh and wiggled

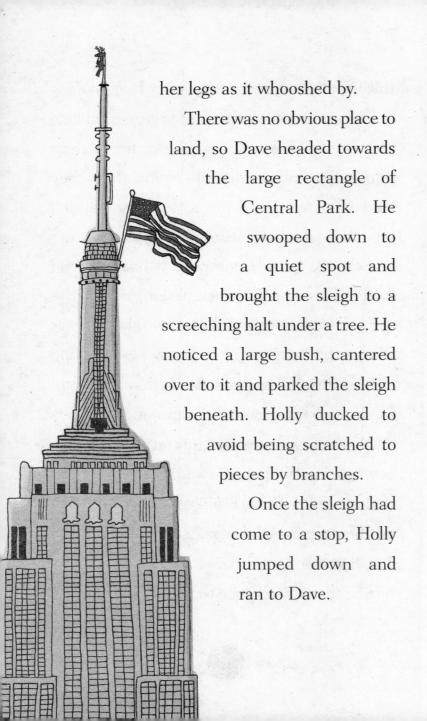

her legs as it whooshed by.

There was no obvious place to land, so Dave headed towards the large rectangle of Central Park. He swooped down to a quiet spot and brought the sleigh to a screeching halt under a tree. He noticed a large bush, cantered over to it and parked the sleigh beneath. Holly ducked to avoid being scratched to pieces by branches.

Once the sleigh had come to a stop, Holly jumped down and ran to Dave.

"Unhook me!" he whispered.

They were aware of traffic in the distance, the wail of sirens, the honking of car horns, but as far as they could tell there was no one nearby.

Holly worked as quickly as she could, but she was still getting used to how the harness worked. Dave, still panting heavily from his exertions, said, "What if someone spots me? A talking reindeer?"

"First thing then," said Holly, "is that you keep your cakehole shut the whole time. The talking bit – we simply can't go there. Other than that, I think we have to embrace the whole reindeer thing. It is Christmas Eve, after all. Let's be confident. It's amazing what you can get away with if you simply act as if you have every right to do what you're doing. Anyway, what choice do we have? Poor Cupid, she looked extremely uncomfortable."

"No talking? What if I need to tell you something?"

"Let's make up a system of signals. Bob your head up and down for yes. Side to side means no. Pawing the ground with your hoof means 'let's get out of here.'"

"I'll snort if I think you've said something dangerous or wrong. Um ... I'll shake my tail if I think you need to be careful."

Holly hopped up on to Dave's back and he trotted towards the south end of the park.

Be confident, thought Holly to herself, wondering how on earth they were going to pull this off.

CHAPTER TWELVE

Walking through Central Park was fine. It was a dark and windy night and people were hurrying back home from work and last-minute Christmas shopping. But Holly and Dave both knew that when they reached the well-lit streets, things would become more interesting.

There was a lot of snow on the ground, and it was extremely cold. Holly was pleased to be wrapped up well.

They passed an ice-skating rink, packed

with skaters. Christmas music blared from the speakers and Holly noticed how many good skaters there were. It felt very Christmassy and Holly suddenly felt a pang for her and her dad's little house back in Great Britain. A house now buried under hundreds and thousands of presents.

They turned on to West 59th Street, and Dave was startled by the noise and the lights. It was one thing swooshing over cities at high speed and quite another being on the ground surrounded by people and cars.

"**Keep going fast!**" shouted Holly. "**The faster we go the harder it is for people to stop and ask us questions.**"

Not knowing which way to go, Dave turned right. There were so many tall buildings in New York City, it was hard to make out where the Empire State Building was. They galloped into Columbus Circle, a roundabout with a monument to Christopher Columbus in the middle, and Dave ran round and round looking for signs for the Empire State Building but couldn't see anything.

They noticed they were being followed by a man with long dark hair on rollerblades. He was dressed in a silver jumpsuit and had a whistle in his mouth, which he was blowing enthusiastically.

"Which way is the Empire State Building?" Holly shouted to the man.

"Follow me!" he yelled and took off down a road that Holly saw was called Broadway.

The traffic was heavy: a river of cars heading slowly in their direction. The rollerblader weaved in and out of the yellow taxis, cars, buses and trucks, sometimes jumping up on to the pavement, dodging cars and pedestrians.

Dave did his best to keep up, but there were a couple of hairy moments. At the junction with 48th Street, a woman was crossing the road with six little yapping dogs on leads as Dave and Holly came tearing past. The sight of a reindeer sent the dogs into a frenzy and they took off after Dave, dragging their unfortunate owner a hundred metres down the road before the dogs gave up, exhausted.

Then as they hared through Times Square, they saw a police officer standing in the middle of the road directing traffic. The rollerblader was travelling backwards at this point, slaloming from side to side. Dave was doing his best to follow when he nearly collided with the cop.

At the last minute, Dave swerved but clipped the police officer as they passed, sending him into a spin. Holly looked back as they galloped off to see the police officer's hat and whistle flying through the air before the cop landed in a confused heap on the ground.

Holly hoped that everything had happened so fast that the police officer wouldn't have been able to take it all in.

Considering she was riding a reindeer down a busy city street, Holly was surprised by how *little* fuss it was causing. Maybe New York City was one of those places where odd things happening just wasn't that odd. People seemed more upset when Holly and Dave ran through red lights, which they did several times.

"Hey," shouted one particularly annoyed man crossing the road. **"I'M WALKIN' HERE!"**

The silver-clad rollerblader took a left and, suddenly, there it was – the Empire State

Building. It towered above them, a magnificent sight. At one time the tallest building in the world and even now, no longer in the top fifty, it was still one of the most famous buildings ever built, visited by millions of tourists each year.

Holly jumped down from Dave's back and said thank you to the rollerblader, who just grinned back, tossed his mane of dark hair, and sped off into the New York night.

Holly and Dave looked up, but the spire wasn't visible from street level. They prayed they weren't too late to save Cupid. They ran into the building and over to the ticket office when Holly suddenly realized they had no money and certainly no dollars. Then Holly had a brainwave.

"Hi," Holly said to the security guard at the turnstiles. "I'm here to deliver Santa's reindeer." She pointed at Dave, who was trying to look relaxed. Not easy when a crowd was forming around them.

"**Why does that cow have antlers?**" asked a little boy.

"**It's not a cow, it's a deer,**" said his gum-chewing mother. "**I hope it doesn't do its business all over the floor.**"

How rude, Dave thought, half tempted to do his business all over the floor just to annoy the woman.

The security guard sighed. Holly had rarely seen anyone who looked so bored before. "**Ya got a pass?**" he said.

"**Santa didn't mention a pass,**" said Holly.

"No pass, no go," the guard said.

"**We're late,**" insisted Holly. "**Please can you let us in? There'll be a lot of disappointed**

125

children otherwise."

"No pass, no go," said the guard, turning to the next in line. "You and your elk need to vamoose."

Holly and Dave decided causing a scene wouldn't help matters. They'd have to think of a different plan.

Walking back on to 34th Street, Dave whispered in her ear, "Elk?"

Holly shot him a look which said *Don't talk!* She motioned up the street and said, "Come on. Let's see if there's another way... Dave?"

Dave had suddenly stopped in his tracks. He indicated across the road, and Holly saw what had grabbed his attention. There was Santa, walking towards the Empire State Building with about a dozen elves in tow. Holly gasped.

"Santa!" she said.

"Not Santa," hissed Dave under his breath. "Are you kidding me? That guy looks nothing like Santa. Santa is super-fit, for one thing. That guy looks like he's got three pillows stuffed up his jacket. And, as for those elves, don't get me started..."

"Sure," said Holly. "Whatever. Stop talking. But they might be our ticket in. Let's hope they are going into the Empire State Building. Follow me."

Holly quickly crossed the road and Dave followed. They fell into line behind "Santa" and the "elves".

Santa walked to the next crossing and pressed the button. The elf at the back casually looked back and saw Dave standing right there behind him.

The elf screamed. All the other elves turned

around and started screaming too. Holly realized they were just children dressed as elves. Some even had fake beards and one had an earring. Holly wondered whether the real Santa allowed his elves to wear earrings.

Dave tossed his head and tried to smile as sweetly as he could. The elves stopped screaming. Santa hadn't seemed to have noticed the kerfuffle, and when the lights changed he crossed the road paying no attention to the commotion going on behind him. The elves, Holly and Dave followed; the elves were now chatting excitedly between themselves about Dave.

Santa walked to a side entrance at the base of the Empire State Building and the elves followed.

"**Remember,**" Holly whispered to Dave,

"confidence!"

Holly and Dave followed the others through the door and the security guard, a different one from before, didn't pay them any heed. Santa walked into a service lift; the elves dutifully followed. There was clearly no room for Dave and Holly in it too.

"We'll get the next one," said Holly to the nearest elf, who was looking at Dave in awe.

The lift doors closed and Holly whispered, **"This is working out beautifully. I'd high-five you if you were able to."**

"All right," said Dave. **"Don't rub it in."**

The lift doors opened and they stepped inside. Holly pressed floor 102.

CHAPTER THIRTEEN

Walking out on to the observation deck of the Empire State Building was a moment Holly was sure she'd remember for the rest of her days. New York stretched out below her in all its glory. A forest of buildings, neatly arranged into a grid; the wide avenues like canyons through which rivers of traffic flowed. It took her breath away.

She was staring at it when she received a nudge from Dave. **"What?"** she said before remembering the reason they were there: Cupid.

Holly looked up and, in the gloom of the wintry night sky, she could just make out a shape attached to the spire.

A metal ladder led upwards from the centre of the deck, but it was fenced off. There was a gate which Holly figured she might be able to crawl underneath.

"I need you to create a distraction," she whispered. **"And I'll go up and see what I can do to help Cupid."**

Dave nodded and casually walked to the other side of the deck. "All I Want for Christmas is You" by Mariah Carey was playing, and Dave began stamping one hoof up and down in time to the music. People – and it was extremely crowded up there with plenty of security guards wandering about – started to take notice. A small crowd gathered around him. As the chorus of the song started, Dave broke out into a full-on tap dance. It was impressive. The crowd cheered and applauded. Clearly no one had seen a tap-dancing reindeer before.

Holly took advantage of everyone looking the other way, quietly slipped under the gate and climbed the ladder.

It led to another smaller deck and another ladder. At the top of this second longer ladder, she reached the bottom of the spike. It was windy up here and Holly was buffeted by the breeze.

She had never been this high up in her life. She'd once heard someone say that when you are up a very tall building, people down on the ground can look like ants. She was so high up she couldn't even make out *any* people below, just the distant lights of cars and an aeroplane flying at what seemed like the same altitude as her. She suddenly felt dizzy and frightened. She gripped the safety rail as tightly as she could and looked up.

The spike itself was swaying in the wind, and there was poor Cupid, legs dangling, unable to move up or down. Below her a huge American flag fluttered and snapped in the stiff breeze.

A ladder led right to the top of the spire. Holly swallowed. She had to do it. She really, really didn't want to, but she had to.

One rung at a time, she told herself, *one rung at a time.*

The ladder had a protective shield around

it, but it didn't give Holly much comfort. She wasn't too bad with heights normally, but this was something else altogether. She took a step up and paused, gripping so tightly her knuckles went white.

Another step. Pause.

Another step. Pause.

Her legs started to shake with fear, so she told herself just to breathe deeply and not look down.

Eventually, after what felt like an hour but was probably only a few minutes, she made it to the top. Cupid had her eyes closed.

"Cupid?" said Holly gently so as not to frighten her. The wind howled.

No response.

"CUPID!" she shouted. That worked. Cupid's eyes opened and she stared in astonishment at the girl.

"Oh, hi," Cupid said, her long eyelashes fluttering. **"Sorry, I was drifting off. It's soooo cold up here. Who are you?"**

"My name's Holly. I'm here with Dave. The new Blitzen? He's down there waiting for us."

Holly explained, as best she could, what had happened that evening. Cupid said she had no idea how she'd ended up here; one minute she was standing on Holly's roof, the next she was hooked around the Empire State Building's spire.

"I'm going to get you down," said Holly.

"That would be marvellous, dear. How?"

"Oh," said Holly. "I hadn't thought of that!"

"I can't climb down this ladder," said Cupid, "so even if you release me from this collar, I'll fall and land on the Observation Deck, which wouldn't be good. I'm fond of my face; I don't want it smushed."

"Don't worry," said Holly unconvincingly, suddenly very worried. "We'll think of something."

"Hope so, darling," said Cupid, smiling softly. She really was extremely beautiful. "This collar is digging into the back of my neck and I'm getting chapped lips."

Holly looked at the flag fluttering below them. "Should we call the fire brigade?"

"If we do that, sweetie, they'll call the

police and they'll have a million questions. No one will believe I ended up here because there was an explosion involving Santa's magic box and your Christmas lights in Great Britain. It doesn't sound likely, does it? They'll keep us for ages and even if they let us go, we'll never find the others in time and Christmas will be cancelled."

Christmas cancelled! thought Holly, her stomach lurching. *That mustn't happen!*

Christmas was too important. Besides, if she couldn't find Santa, she had no hope of finding Dad.

If only we had something to work with, she thought. *A rope or sheet or*—

"I've got an idea!" she exclaimed. "It's a risk, though."

"A risk is what we have to take," said Cupid.

"What's the idea?"

"If you can't climb down the ladder and you can't drop, you'll have to float!"

"Excuse me?" said Cupid.

"Float!" Holly smiled. "Parachute!"

"Have you got a parachute with you? That's impressive planning, darling!"

"No," said Holly, "but we can make one using that massive flag. We can let the wind do the heavy lifting. I'll tie the four corners to your four hooves, wait for the wind to fill it and lift it above your head like a parachute, then release the harness and you'll float down to the Observation Deck. We'll untie you, grab Dave, get in the lift and down we go!"

Cupid gulped. "Wow!" She stared out across the sparkling New York skyline. "Not sure what to say. I suppose we don't have much choice.

It's worth a try. You can tie strong knots?"

"Absolutely!"

"And I'll be landing upside down?"

"I'm afraid so."

"Well, darling," said Cupid, "go for it!" She smiled encouragingly at Holly. Or as encouragingly as she could given that she was hanging from a spire over one hundred floors above the ground.

Holly carefully climbed down the ladder and ran over to the flag. It was cracking in what now felt like a gale. Two knots held it in place. Holly undid the first one but stopped and thought before undoing the second. The last thing she wanted was for the wind to carry her off into the night sky.

It was a huge flag and that would make it a good parachute, but it also meant it was a handful to control. Carefully, she untied each knot and made her way over to Cupid with it.

Fighting the wind, she tied each of the two outside corners to Cupid's back two hooves.

Once done, the flag filled with air and tried to float away.

"The wind's too strong!" shouted Holly.

"You're doing great," encouraged Cupid.

Holly waited for a few seconds, hoping the wind might die down a little. And her patience was rewarded.

"Hurry!" shouted Cupid.

Holly worked as quickly as she could, attaching the last two corners to Cupid's front hooves. When both were in place, the wind filled the flag and it lifted into the air.

The only thing keeping Cupid from floating was the harness attached to the spire.

Holly unbuckled it, waited for the wind to fill the flag-parachute above Cupid's head, then released her.

For a second, Cupid hung in the air. Time seemed to stand still. Cupid, upside down, looked at Holly and Holly looked at Cupid. Then a big gust of wind swept Cupid higher into the air, the flag billowing and snapping noisily in the breeze, and suddenly the reindeer was gone, lifted up and off into the New York night sky, climbing higher and higher and moving at tremendous speed.

CHAPTER FOURTEEN

Holly watched Cupid go, rigid with shock. What had she done?

She had to find Dave. He'd know what to do. Hopefully.

Down the three ladders and she was back on the Observation Deck. She rolled under the gate and looked for her reindeer friend.

He wasn't there.

She grabbed the first person she could. **"Have you seen my reindeer, please?"**

"理解できない," replied the startled Japanese tourist.

"Sorry!" said Holly, turning to a family of Swedes. "Have you seen a reindeer?"

"What is this rain you are speaking about, dear?"

"Never mind!" said Holly, running to a security guard. He told her that, yes, the reindeer was gone. He'd been ordered to leave the building for tap-dancing without a permit.

"Good dancer, gotta say," said the guard. "Impressive. Inspired me to start taking lessons again. I used to tap-dance as a kid but then, well, I don't know what happened really, I got interested in other things and I stopped going. Always regretted that. I could have been a star..."

"Thanks, bye!" shouted Holly, cutting him

off. She didn't have time to listen to this man's life story.

Holly ran to the lift, pressing the button repeatedly, willing the lift to arrive.

All the way down, she panicked. What was she going to do now? She'd lost both reindeer!

She sprang from the lift and ran to the exit. There was no sign of Dave.

The streets were even busier than before, and Holly wasn't that tall, so she found it difficult to see beyond the people immediately around her. She threw her head back and started shouting, **"DAVE! DAVE! DAVE!"**

Two workmen on their way home heard and joined in: **"DAVE! DAVE!"**

A group of nuns walking past joined in too. **"DAVE! DAVE! DAVE!"** they yelled in unison, smiling at Holly. The doorman of the hotel across the street got involved and soon it seemed like everyone in the area was shouting **"DAVE!"**. No one had any idea why they were shouting it and, by this stage, who had started it, but, well, it was Christmas Eve in New York, weirder things happen.

And then:

"Holly!"

Holly saw Dave balancing on a fire hydrant on the other side of the road, looking for her in the melee. She could have screamed with relief. Holly ran over.

"Where's Cupid?" asked Dave.

Holly looked up and there, a speck in the night sky, was Cupid, still attached to the flag, floating away. **"That's her!"** she said, pointing. **"Come on! You run; I'll track her."**

"I'm not even going to ask what's going

on," said Dave, as Holly leapt on to his back. **"Just tell me which way to go. Pull my left ear to turn me left and my right one to turn me right."**

With Holly on his back, Dave took off as fast as he could.

For the first few minutes it seemed as though Cupid was getting further and further away, but then the wind dropped again and they gained on her.

Dave zigzagged through the traffic which seemed to be mostly at a standstill. A couple of times Dave had to jump up and over cars, his hooves clattering across their roofs, startling the drivers and passengers inside.

Cupid was getting lower and lower in the sky. Holly was worried she'd hit one of the skyscrapers she was flying towards. It would all be Holly's fault…

Holly realized they were galloping through quiet darkness now. The park! The ice-skating rink! Which meant the sleigh was nearby…

"Um, Holly?" said Dave. "Look."

Holly looked and there was Cupid, at the mercy of the wind, swinging wildly back and forth as the breeze came and went, flying in sideways, and landing with a bump on the ice of the skating rink, skidding right across it from one side to the other, the huge Stars and Stripes flag following behind, gathering up dozens of skaters in its wake. When Cupid came to a stop, there was a pile of skaters thrashing about on the ice behind her, wrapped in the American flag.

Holly ran to untie Cupid and, before the skaters were able to untangle themselves from the flag and from each other, the three of them ran off towards the sleigh, giggling hysterically. The sheer relief had sent them giddy with joy.

Holly quickly hooked them up to the sleigh and put the box in **FLIGHT MODE**. They were airborne in moments, streaking at speed into the sky. Holly sunk back into her chair, flooded with relief and wondering where this adventure was going to take her next.

CHAPTER FIFTEEN

Given that they had no idea where the other reindeer or Santa or Holly's dad were, they decided to go back to Holly's house.

The journey back was as exhilarating as the one out to New York, and there was so much to wonder and marvel at, it didn't give Holly time to reflect too much on the task that lay ahead.

As they neared home, though, their relief wore off and worry began to set in. Holly couldn't help wonder if Cupid was right and

Christmas would be ruined. Would she end up being the *only* reindeer they managed to rescue? Would there be no more presents delivered across the world tonight? And what about Dad?

Dave put his head down and flew in silence. He felt guilty about his part in this mess, and he was going to do everything he could to sort it out. But how? They tore through the night sky and soon Holly's house appeared in front of them. They landed as best they could without damaging anything on the huge pile of presents under which the house lay.

As they slid to a stop, Holly heard a car driving into the cul-de-sac below. *Uh-oh,* thought Holly, *who's this?* She motioned for the others to be still and quiet and they listened.

The car parked outside one of the houses across the road and they heard two doors open and shut.

"What on earth is all this?" said one, a woman.

Mrs Throat-Badger, thought Holly, *they've seen the mountain of presents and come to investigate! They'll call the police! The fire brigade! The army! The—*

"Look what Simon's done now!" said her husband, Mr Throat-Badger. **"Every Christmas he gets more and more carried away! What's he like?!"**

"Ridiculous," said his wife. **"As if the lights weren't enough! What a totally over-the-top display."**

"I quite like it."

"Thierry!" scolded Mrs Throat-Badger. "I forbid you to like it. It's naff, naff, *naff.*"

"I think it's cool. That must have taken *a lot* of work. Wonder how they get in and out of the house?"

"I suppose it's better than all the lights. I'm going in. It's cold."

"Righto."

They went inside and Holly breathed a sigh of relief.

"Now what?" she asked.

"Check the magic box again. See if there's any new info."

So Holly flipped open the magic box and went through the list again:

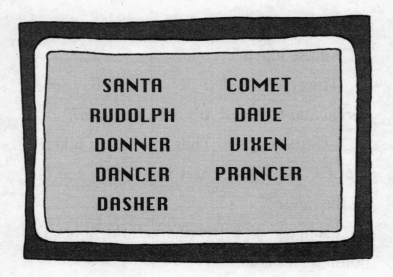

SANTA COMET
RUDOLPH DAVE
DONNER VIXEN
DANCER PRANCER
DASHER

Santa: nothing.

Rudolph: nothing.

Donner: nothing.

Holly sighed. Why was this proving so difficult? The magic box had tracked down Cupid to such a specific place, why couldn't it manage the rest?

Dasher: nothing.

Pressing Comet, though, brought the spinning Earth back on to the screen, and

Holly's heart leapt.

Across America, over the Pacific Ocean, Asia and Europe spun the globe before it slowed down over the Atlantic Ocean.

"Uh-oh," said Holly to Cupid and Dave. **"Hope you can swim!"**

But as the image zoomed in, it also moved northwards, across the north Atlantic, over Greenland, and settled on a white piece of snow somewhere inside the Arctic Circle.

"Not far from the North Pole! I'd better get some more clothes on!" said Holly.

"How are you going to get into the house?" said Dave, looking at the mountain of presents blocking the way.

"Good point," said Holly. **"I suppose I managed in New York, and it was very cold there. How much colder can it be in the Arctic Circle?"**

Cupid and Dave looked at each other. "Um, quite a bit colder," said Cupid. "But the sleigh is heated so…"

"Yes, let's go for it," said Holly. "Comet might need our help urgently, after all."

Into the magic box went the coordinates, **FLIGHT MODE** was selected, Cupid and Dave leapt forward, and in no time they were up, up and away.

CHAPTER SIXTEEN

Like New York, it was night-time in the Arctic Circle. In fact, at this time of the year the sun didn't rise *at all* for months and wouldn't show itself again until late March.

Unlike New York, there were no streetlights to help illuminate the scene for them. There were no lights at all for hundreds and hundreds of miles. Luckily, the moon was out in the cloudless night, casting an eerie silvery light over the wilderness, while a dazzling sweep of stars shone above.

They faithfully followed the coordinates set by the magic box and touched down on the ice on a slight slope. Once they had come to a stop, they listened intently as their eyes adjusted to the darkness.

Holly didn't feel cold at all, so that was something. She wondered whether she would be all right if she stepped out of the sleigh, given the others had told her that the temperature in the Arctic could be dangerously low.

The thing that startled and surprised Holly was the noise the ice made. A creaking, squeaking, groaning noise that changed from moment to moment as the sea ice moved and shifted. Vast ice floes rubbed up against each other, grumbling and moaning, with an occasional boom or cracking noise, sometimes with a high-pitched whine. The sleigh trembled and shook as the ice beneath them shuddered and rolled. It was such a strange sensation to be on something constantly moving and shifting like that. Were they safe?

Would a gap in the ice open up and suddenly plunge them into the deadly waters below? It was certainly anything but relaxing; Holly gripped the arms of her chair tightly.

Without warning, the sleigh jerked backwards. Caught off guard, Holly was thrown forwards off the armchair and on to the front of the sleigh, hitting her forehead on the wooden frame. She scrambled back into her chair and rubbed her head.

"What happened there?" she asked. **"That hurt."**

Before a reply came from either Cupid or Dave, it happened again. A violent lurch backwards and Holly slid forward off the chair.

Why doesn't this thing have a seat belt? she wondered.

"Hey!" she shouted. **"Is that you? What are**

you doing?"

There was no response from either Cupid or Dave, but beyond them, from out of the murky darkness, came the sound of a hoarse panting, rough and loud and deep. It sounded like a giant dog clearing its throat over and over.

The sleigh jerked back again, and Holly understood now that it was Cupid and Dave backing up that was causing the sleigh to move. What were they retreating from? What was out there?

"Dave!" hissed Holly. **"What's happening?"**

The ice continued to creak and groan, but Dave and Cupid said nothing.

Then, poking its head around a huge lump of ice in front of them, Holly could see what Dave and Cupid were backing away from.

Wet blonde fur, two small dark eyes, powerful

shoulders, mouth hanging open to reveal a huge tongue coated in a gooey white slop, two big yellowing teeth jutting up from the front corners of its bottom jaw, head low and lolling from side to side, an enormous and malevolent-looking polar bear swaggered towards them.

Holly froze. She opened her mouth to say something, but no sound came out. It wasn't just the size of the bear that alarmed her, it was something about the look in its eyes: blank, dead. The hairs stood up on the back of Holly's neck.

Cupid and Dave continued to edge backwards.

The bear stopped and peered back over its shoulder at something behind it. Cupid and Dave continued to back up but more smoothly than before. Trying to move away from the bear as gently as possible so as not to alarm it.

The bear swung back to face them and let out a low rumbling growl and then opened its mouth wide and roared. Holly was so astonished she let out a little laugh before a bolt of fear shot through her.

Then from just wide of the bear, out of the gloom, came a reindeer – Comet! He zigzagged around the polar bear, Dave and Cupid and leapt in one powerful bound over Holly's head and into the sleigh.

At the same time, Cupid and Dave jumped to their right and took off across the snow and ice. Holly just managed to hang on to the chair this time but was thrown wildly from side to side.

The bear had stopped roaring. Holly dared to look back and saw that the animal had taken off after the sleigh and was not far behind it and gaining, its small beady eyes fixed on Holly. She looked down at Comet trying to scrabble to his feet on the smooth and slippery wooden floor of the sleigh.

Dave was shouting something. Holly turned

back to the front.

"**What?**" she shouted back. "**What did you say, Dave?**"

"**FLIGHT MODE!**" she heard him yell.

Of course, they needed to get into the air!

She flicked open the lid of the magic box and tried to type in the username **SANTA1** but the sleigh was bouncing all over the place and it came out as **SDSAFC@!**. She deleted and tried again.

SNRTS1

Again.

SANTSQ

Panic surged through her. She tried desperately to remain calm. She could hear the heavy thump of the bear's paws as they lolloped at her back. Again, she told herself, try again.

SANTA1

Yes! She had managed it. Now for the password.

But the sleigh lurched suddenly to the left and the magic box slid off its plinth. She lunged to try to grab it, but it tumbled off into the darkness. She heard a thud as it landed on the ice and watched as the polar bear slowed to inspect the curious glowing item.

Oh no.

"Stop! The magic box!" Holly felt like sobbing.

Dave and Cupid wheeled around in a big arc to face the bear. Comet had managed to stagger to his feet, his strong shoulders rising and falling as he gulped down huge lungfuls of freezing Arctic air.

"I'll get the bear to chase me," he said in his

low gentle voice. "You circle back, rescue the box and come back for me."

"Are you sure, Comet?" asked Cupid.

"What choice do we have?" asked Comet.

"I could do it," volunteered Dave.

"No," said Comet. "You're all harnessed up. It would take too long. I'll jump out and go left, you go right. The bear will follow me. Collect the box, then come back for me."

Cupid and Dave looked at each other. Holly said nothing. She felt that this was all her fault; she was the one in charge of the box, but this was no time for self-pity or apology.

"All right," said Cupid. "Please be careful, angel."

They looked back at the polar bear who was nudging the box with its nose.

"Quick, before the bear stands on the box

and breaks it," said Comet.

He jumped out of the sleigh. The ice around them moaned and creaked.

"Ready," said Comet. **"Go!"**

He trotted to his left, eyes fixed on the bear. Cupid and Dave quietly pulled the sleigh to the right.

Holly sat as still as she could, her heart in her mouth. If anything happened to the magic box, how would they get home? Never mind Christmas, at this point she didn't want to even think about being stuck in the Arctic Circle in the middle of winter with only three talking reindeer and an angry polar bear for company. She could feel the cold creeping over her. Without the box there would be no heating either, it seemed. How long could she survive in this environment?

When they were about thirty metres apart, Comet bellowed and the polar bear looked up.

The bear eyed Comet disdainfully and decided the glowing magic box was more interesting than a big-eyed reindeer. He batted it with an enormous paw and sent it skidding across the ice. It bumped and rattled. Holly winced.

Comet bellowed again and stepped bravely towards the polar bear. This time the bear paid attention. Lowering its head menacingly, it began to shuffle towards Comet. Then it broke into a run. Comet started to run too, but then something unexpected happened. The bear veered sharply left, ignoring Comet and heading straight for Cupid, Dave and Holly.

This was not the plan.

Cupid and Dave began to gallop across the uneven surface. The sleigh bounced and hopped around behind them, and Holly clung on as though her life depended on it. Which it did. If she were thrown from the sleigh, she'd be the bear's lunch.

There was no question the polar bear was getting closer. He was astonishingly fast because Cupid and Dave were no slouches. Holly looked around for something to throw at the bear, but there was only the armchair she was sitting in, and she couldn't lift that, could she?

Closer and closer drew the bear; it was relentless. Soon only a couple of metres separated the bear from the back of the sleigh. Up ahead Holly could see something that made her stomach turn – water! The ice stopped and water began. She shouted to Dave and Cupid, but they didn't respond. It was probably too noisy for them to hear.

Holly stood up to shout but sat down again quickly as they hit a small bump and she nearly went flying. She looked back to the bear and as she did, she saw Comet careering towards them all at top speed. Dave looked to his right and saw Comet coming too. It looked to Holly as though Comet was going to collide with the side of the sleigh.

At the last second, Comet leapt into the air, landing on his side, skidding across the ice with his two upper hooves waving wildly, a huge grin on his face. He slid like this neatly between the sleigh and the bear. At the same moment Dave and Cupid veered sharply right.

The bear, faced with a gurning reindeer flashing across his vision one way and the sleigh darting the other, was utterly baffled. He tripped on a lump of hard ice sticking out of the ground, fell flat on his belly and slid with little grace for thirty metres, straight into the freezing waters of the Arctic Ocean, hitting the water with an almighty *splosh*.

Comet though, was also heading dangerously close to the water's edge. Rather than try to get back on his feet, he cleverly used his antlers like a brake, throwing his head back and jamming them into the ice behind him. Showers of snow and ice sprayed everywhere as he came to a grinding halt.

Dave and Cupid turned so sharply that the sleigh tilted over, lifting one of its runners right off the ground. Holly clung to the right-hand arm of the chair. As one side of the sleigh lifted, her body flew out – the only thing keeping her from flying off was her grip on this arm.

Comet and Cupid slowed slightly, allowing the sleigh to clatter back on to the snow and Holly to set herself the right way round in the chair. They pulled up next to the magic box.

Holly jumped out and gingerly picked it up. She put it back on its plinth. With her heart in her mouth, she opened it up. For a second nothing happened and then it flickered to life. Holly quickly typed in the username and password and put it in **FLIGHT MODE**.

In the distance they could see the bedraggled polar bear pulling itself out of the water and staring moodily at them. Holly wondered whether the bear would have the stomach to chase them all over again but, rather than stay and find out, they decided not to waste any time hooking Comet up to the sleigh. He jumped in behind Holly, and soon Dave and Cupid were pulling them all high into the dark Arctic sky, looking down on a confused and very, very wet polar bear.

CHAPTER SEVENTEEN

There were no further updates on the whereabouts of anyone else, so they headed back to Holly's house.

Landing beside the house covered in presents, Holly wanted nothing more than to be sitting in her living room, drinking hot chocolate and opening presents on Christmas morning with her dad. It was her favourite moment of the year, and even though it should only be a few hours away, it felt like a complete impossibility.

They had three tired reindeer. But they had no Santa.

The sleigh came to a halt. As they sat there catching their breath, they heard a car pulling up in the street. Holly motioned for Comet to be quiet although he didn't need telling.

They listened as two car doors opened and shut.

"What on earth is all this?" said a woman.

Mrs Throat-Badger, thought Holly, *again?!*

"Look what Simon's done now!" said Mr Throat-Badger. **"Every Christmas he gets more and more carried away! What's he like?!"**

"Ridiculous," said his wife. **"As if the lights weren't enough! What a totally over-the-top display."**

"I quite like it."

"Thierry!" scolded

Mrs Throat-Badger. "**I forbid you to like it. It's naff, naff, *naff.*"

"**I think** it's cool. That must have taken *a lot* of work. **Wonder how they get in and out of the house?**"

"**I suppose it's better than all the lights. I'm going in. It's cold.**"

"**Righto.**"

Once the door to the Throat-Badger house had closed, Holly dared to speak.

"**Isn't that the exact same conversation they had last time?**" she whispered to Dave.

Dave nodded, as stunned as Holly was.

"**Why are they repeating themselves?**" he asked her. "**It doesn't make sense.**"

"**It's the box, angel,**" said Cupid, batting her super-long eyelashes. "**It can play with time. That's how Santa gets around the world to**

177

every house in one night. It must be helping us out. Check the box again, Holly, see if it can tell us where any more of the reindeer are."

Once again, the box only seemed to know the location of one reindeer, Dasher. As the image of the Earth spun, Holly said, **"It's almost like it's guiding us to them one at a time."**

"Wouldn't surprise me," said Comet as the image spun past America and Asia and Europe and back across America again. **"That box will have worked out what's best."**

Once again, the map started to slow over water, but this time the water was the Pacific Ocean. Right in the middle of the Pacific Ocean.

"There's nothing there, right?" said a shocked Holly as the image zoomed in.

"Well, only ..." muttered Cupid as the image

moved closer and closer, "... Tahiti..."

And, sure enough, the screen settled on the island of Tahiti.

"**Dasher's on Tahiti?**" Cupid laughed. "*Of course* **he is! The absolute rascal.**"

"**What do you mean?**" asked Holly.

"**Oh, you'll find out,**" said Comet. "**We should go. The box helped us out this time by jumping time backwards, but we shouldn't rely on that. If sunlight hits your house, Holly, before we get all the reindeer and Santa back, then it's all over.**"

"Yes," said Holly. "I know. Let's go."

"**You can harness me up,**" said Comet, jumping out of the sleigh. As he landed, he called out with a sharp cry of pain.

"**What's wrong?**" asked Holly, alarmed.

"**Nothing,**" said Comet, wincing. "**I'm fine.**"

But he was clearly not fine. Holly ran to the side of the sleigh. Cupid and Dave strained to see what was happening.

"My shoulder," said Comet quietly to Holly. **"Something happened to my shoulder on the ice."**

Comet looked downcast. Holly could feel he was embarrassed to be injured and had been trying to hide it.

"Let's get you into the house," said Holly. **"We need to rest that shoulder."**

"How?" asked Dave. **"The house is completely buried under this mountain of Christmas presents."**

"That's not a problem, sweetie," said Cupid. **"Use the magic box to deal with that."**

Holly ran to the box and logged in.

"Go to CLEAN, then PRESENT CHAMBER 1,

then ORGANIZE."

Comet, breathing heavily, closed his eyes. Holly worked her way through the different screens as instructed and when she pressed **ORGANIZE**, something remarkable happened. The presents beneath them snapped into an entirely different formation. Now, instead of looking like they'd just been dropped haphazardly from a great height, they were arranged into neat rows and columns, larger presents at the bottom, smaller ones at the top. There was a long sweeping staircase leading from where the sleigh was down to the front garden and a neat pathway cleared to the front door.

Holly looked at Dave and Cupid, astonished.

"What can I say, duckie?" drawled Cupid. **"That box is the real hero of Christmas. Now, Comet, my little love vomit, are you able to**

walk down to the house?"

"I'll try," said the big strong reindeer and began to limp down. He was clearly in huge pain.

"Unhook me, chickadee," said Cupid to Holly. "I'd better stay with him. I used to be a nurse. Will you two be all right on your own?"

Holly and Dave looked at each other. This was a blow. They felt much more reassured having experienced reindeer with them. Still, what could they do?

"We'll be fine," said Holly, untying Cupid.

"Be smart out there," said Cupid. "You won't have the advantage of operating in the dark on Tahiti. It's currently midday there. There'll be nowhere to hide."

Holly felt like saying *how can we possibly get away with a flying reindeer and Santa's sleigh*

in broad daylight, but she decided to keep her thoughts to herself. However, a quick glance at Dave made her feel she wasn't the only nervous one.

Cupid began to help Comet towards the house. Holly placed the magic box into **FLIGHT MODE**, gave Dave the signal and within moments the two of them hurtled skywards. Destination: Tahiti.

CHAPTER EIGHTEEN

They landed on the slopes of a big wooded hill on the eastern side of the small island. There were too many people around to make it safe to land anywhere else. They checked the magic box – apparently Dasher was on Toaroto Beach.

"I think you might have to do this alone, Holly," Dave said. "I'm worried I'd be too easily spotted."

Holly nodded. She took off her warm hat, gloves and coat and left them in the sleigh. "OK. I've got the coordinates. If I'm not back in two hours, come and find me."

"You'll be brilliant," said Dave. "If I had thumbs, I'd give you a thumbs up."

"Bit weird, but thanks," said Holly. "I know what you mean."

Dave tried to give her a reassuring wink.

"You OK, Dave?" asked Holly.

"Just trying to wink," said Dave. "Now, off you go. No time to lose. Find Dasher – and don't stand for any of his nonsense. He needs a firm hand."

Holly grinned as best she could and set

off, glancing back five or six times before she disappeared around the first bend and out of sight of Dave.

It was a hot, humid day and the sun was as high in the sky as it would get. The hillside was steep and densely covered with trees and shrubs. There was loads of greenery everywhere, which made Holly think it must rain a lot. Holly hated being in the rain and prayed it wouldn't; she didn't like getting wet.

"Places that are very green need a lot of rain otherwise they wouldn't be green," her dad always told her when it rained, as though that would make her feel any better about getting wet.

Down the road she tramped, heading towards the sea.

Holly laughed at the idea that they could

travel in Santa's sleigh at unbelievable speeds right to the very edge of space, then hurtle down to an island on the other side of the planet, in the middle of the biggest ocean; that they could work out where Dasher was with incredible precision – but that the last bit of the journey had to be Holly walking on her own down a big hill in the afternoon heat. *Sometimes magic and technology only take you so far,* she thought. In the end a bit of hard work was still necessary to finish the job.

She was tired and thirsty, but she kept putting one foot in front of the other. She didn't see a single other person on the road, no cars, no pedestrians. Sometimes a colourful parrot would burst squawking noisily from the trees, but other than that she was on her own.

Are there snakes here? she wondered. Holly was not a fan of snakes.

After what felt like ages, she was finally getting close to the sea. She could smell it. That unmistakable smell that reminded her of days at the beach when she was younger: building sandcastles and moats in the sand with her dad.

Following the path downhill, the trees opened up and there it was: the Pacific Ocean. Holly didn't pay it much attention. She was on a mission. She had to find Dasher. In only a few short hours, it would be Christmas morning.

The beach was sandy and long. Really long. Worryingly long. It also appeared to be completely empty.

She kicked off her shoes and socks. Walking on a beach in shoes and socks was weird and should be illegal, she believed. The absolute best thing about walking down a beach was getting to do so in your bare feet. Sand and bare feet were a match made in heaven.

She walked and she walked. There was no sign of anyone. Where was Dasher? She started to run, trying to contain her alarm.

It was hot and she would have loved to go for a swim, but she knew she couldn't. There was no time, and she had no idea what was in those waters. Sharks? She reckoned the warm waters here would be full of *massive* sharks.

Then she noticed a spot where the sand had been disturbed. She inspected it. A trail of what looked suspiciously like hoofprints in the sand, leading away from the sea towards the trees that fringed the beach.

She followed them away from the pounding

sea towards a line of palm trees that ran along the beach and, there, strung between two of the trees – a hammock.

There was something in the hammock too, a big bulge that caused the hammock to sag low. Very low. Whatever was in the hammock

was extremely heavy. And whatever was inside the hammock had pulled the hammock material over its head so that it was hidden from view.

"Dasher?" said Holly in a clear and confident voice.

"Yes?" said the body in the hammock. Then after a second: "I mean no. I'm not Dasher."

"If you're not Dasher, why did you say yes first?"

"I was just being polite."

"It's nice to be polite," said Holly.

"It is," said the voice.

"Right," said Holly. "If you're not Dasher, I'll leave you alone."

"Great."

"Bye then, Dasher."

"Bye," said the voice.

There was a pause.

"But I'm not Dasher," it said.

"You are, though, aren't you?"

"OK, I am," said Dasher. "Bye then."

"Dasher, I'm here with Dave. We've come to take you back. We need you. If we don't get all the reindeer and Santa back before the sun rises on my house, then Christmas will be cancelled. So will you please come with me?"

"I don't want to," said Dasher from inside his hammock cocoon.

"Why not?"

"Because look at this place! Look at it! No one told me there were places like this. It's *amazing*. I've spent my whole life in freezing places. Lapland is so cold. Here it's warm. You can see whales passing in the distance. Whales! Just over there! And it's so relaxing. I've discovered

I'm *very* good at relaxing. I want to stay."

"All right, look," said Holly, trying to remain calm. "I need to find my dad. I care about Christmas, obviously, everyone does, but I care about my dad more. If we don't sort this situation out, I might never see him again." She took a deep breath. "So, I get it, I get that it's hot here and you can watch whales and swing about in a hammock and everything, but I need to collect all the reindeer for Santa's sleigh because the magic box is only giving me information about one reindeer at a time for some reason, and you are the next reindeer I need to collect, so I'm collecting you whether you like it or not."

There was silence from the hammock. Holly looked to the sky and bit her lip. She wanted to control her temper. She was hot and tired and thirsty and hungry, and this reindeer was being a pest.

"**The thing is**," Dasher said eventually, "**I think there's been a mistake. My name *is* Dasher. But I'm not a reindeer.**"

"**Really?**" said Holly. "**What are you then?**"

"**I'm … a…**"

"**Yes?**"

"**I'm a chicken.**"

Holly opened up the top of the hammock. Inside, on his back, lay Dasher. He had garlands of flowers hanging about his head, a colourful iced drink in a big glass with a straw and a little umbrella sticking out of it. On his belly was a small guitar.

The main thing Holly noticed, though, was that Dasher was, most definitely and without any shadow of a doubt, a reindeer and not a

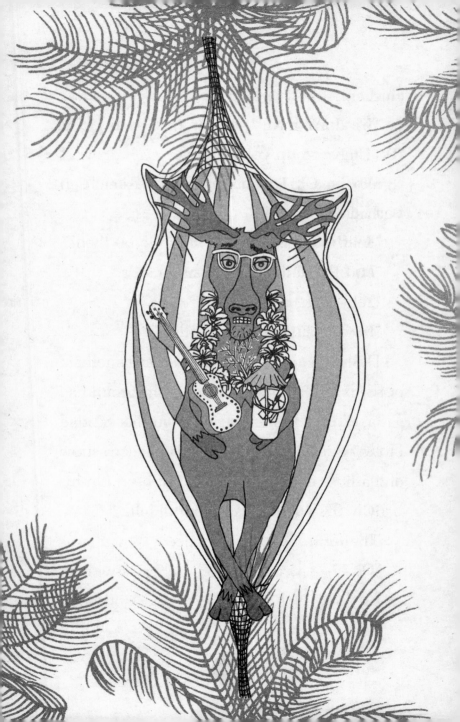

chicken.

"We don't have time for this," said Holly. "Do I have to tip you out?"

"No, no, OK, I'm coming," said Dasher. "Can you hold my drink?"

Holly took his drink.

"And the guitar?" said Dasher.

Holly took the guitar.

"Now I'll just very carefully…"

Dasher leant over and then clumsily fell out of the hammock into a heap on the ground.

"You're carrying me on your back," said Holly, who was not prepared to take any more of Dasher's nonsense.

"Oh, OK. As long as it's not uphill…"

"It's uphill."

"Oh."

CHAPTER NINETEEN

The whole flight home, with Dasher grumbling alongside him as they pulled the sleigh, Dave was frantically making calculations.

It had taken Holly about four and a half hours to find Dasher and get him back to the sleigh. Which meant it should still be nighttime back at her house. The sun didn't rise until after eight a.m. at that time of year and they had left at about midnight. All should be well for now, but there were still lots of reindeer to collect. Without the help of the magic box, they would eventually run out of time.

Landing back at the house, they were relieved to find it still dark, but the big question was whether the magic box had turned back time again. They slid to a stop and waited.

A few seconds later, the car drew up across the road and Mrs Throat-Badger and her husband got out.

"What on earth is all this?" said Mrs Throat-Badger.

"Look what Simon's done now!" said Mr Throat-Badger. **"Every Christmas he gets more and more carried away! What's he like?!"**

"Ridiculous," said his wife. **"As if the lights weren't enough! What a totally over-the-top display."**

"I quite like it."

"Thierry!" scolded Mrs Throat-Badger. "I forbid you to like it. It's naff, naff, *naff.*"

"I think it's cool. That must have taken *a lot* of work. Wonder how they get in and out of the house?"

"I suppose it's better than all the lights. I'm going in. It's cold."

"Righto."

Dave and Holly exchanged looks of relief. All was well.

Dasher had done nothing but moan the whole way back, so Holly decided to leave him at the house with Cupid and Comet.

"Right," Holly said, when Dasher had trotted inside to join Cupid and Comet and the two Mrs Ditherses. "Let's see where we're going next, shall we? I wonder why the magic box is only telling us where the reindeer are one at a time."

"It must have a reason," said Dave.

Holly fired up the box and the names appeared on the screen.

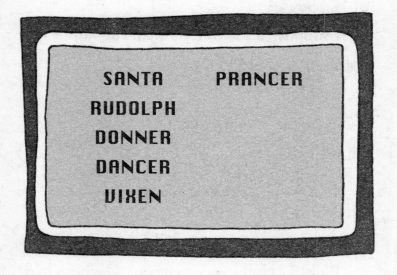

SANTA   PRANCER
RUDOLPH
DONNER
DANCER
VIXEN

Holly, as usual, tried Santa first but, again, there was no joy there. Nothing for Rudolph, but Donner's search brought up the spinning globe on the screen. She waited with bated breath. The image zoomed in.

"Tokyo!" exclaimed Holly to Dave. "I've always wanted to go to Japan! Let's go and get Donner!"

CHAPTER TWENTY

It was morning in Japan: Christmas morning.
And, as Japan was one of the first countries
Santa delivered presents to on his rounds, Dave
had already been there earlier. Most cities look
alike at night flying at that speed, but Tokyo
was memorable because of its size.

Tokyo is the biggest city in the world; it
spreads out over an enormous distance and is
home to more than thirty-nine million people.
That's bigger than London or New York.

Holly and Dave knew that there would be nowhere to hide.

They also knew that Japan is a place that loves technology and was often where exciting new inventions are first seen. The plan was to be bold and fly right to where Donner was. If people noticed them, hopefully they would assume that this was some exciting invention being unveiled for the first time.

Donner, according to the magic box, was in a zoo, Ueno Zoo, in a part of Tokyo called Hino City. Hopefully, it being Christmas Day, the zoo would be closed to visitors, giving Dave and Holly a better chance of dropping in unobserved. Whether Donner was in a cage or not, they had no idea.

Holly and Dave tore out of the cloudy morning Tokyo sky and swooped down over Ueno Zoo, landing safely just inside. The zoo was indeed closed, which was good.

"There will be zookeepers around, though," warned Holly. "So keep an eye out."

"I'll keep hooked up to the sleigh," suggested Dave. "That way if anyone does see us, we can pretend this is a Christmas thing for the zoo."

"Good idea," said Holly. "And it'll mean a quick getaway if we need one."

Dave started to drag the sleigh through the zoo looking for Donner. The sleigh was designed to be flown through the air or pulled over snow. It was certainly *not* designed to be dragged over concrete and it made quite a racket. Dave was also worried about the big crack down its side. Was it getting bigger or was that his imagination?

He decided to ignore it and hope for the best. There wasn't much they could do about it here.

On their left were some colourful-looking

birds and a pagoda, a traditional Japanese building which looked like five square roofs placed on top of each other. Beside it were what Holly recognized as deer.

"Look, deer!" she said as quietly as she could to Dave. "They might know where Donner is?"

"Because they are deer?" said Dave crossly. "You think we all know each other because we look vaguely similar?"

"No," said Holly. "I just thought you could ask them."

"No, I can't ask them," said Dave. "They are Japanese Sika deer. They're really cool and I'm shy. Besides, we don't speak the same language."

"Fine!" she said. "I'll ask them then."

She jumped down off the sleigh and went over to the deer. Three of them came to the edge of their enclosure.

"Hi," said Holly. She remembered she was in Japan, so she bowed. To her astonishment, the deer bowed back.

"Nice to meet you," she continued. "I don't suppose you've seen a reindeer? She's called Donner and she looks like him."

Holly pointed at Dave. The Sika deer stared at her and said nothing.

Holly put her hands up to try and impersonate antlers. "Reindeer?"

She ran around a little and tried to impersonate a deer bellowing with her hands forming antlers. When there was absolutely no response from the Sika deer, Holly felt silly.

"Never mind," she said. "Thank you. Bye."

Holly ran back to the sleigh.

"Well that was embarrassing," said Dave as they headed further into the zoo.

They passed red pandas, two enormous bison and three elephants. As they moved by each cage or enclosure, the animals inside came silently to the front to inspect the sleigh. They saw llamas and tapirs and capybaras. There were emus and penguins and lemurs and flamingos. Kangaroos. An okapi, chewing on something, blinked slowly and watched them pass.

"There she is!" said Dave suddenly. **"Over there!"**

Holly followed his gaze and, yes, a reindeer stood in an enclosure that had a Japanese sign above it with the words **ANIMALS OF ASIA** underneath.

"Donner?" called out Holly.

Donner came up to the concrete ditch that separated the enclosure from the public areas.

She looked about her fearfully, then nodded.

"How do we get you out?" Holly asked.

Donner indicated a zookeeper's hut. Holly approached it cautiously and looked in through the open window. Inside, a man sat on a chair, his head laid on the desk in front of him. He was fast asleep. Behind him on the wall was a rack of keys, all labelled in Japanese.

Holly despaired. Even if she were able to sneak in and get to the key rack without waking the zookeeper, how would she know which key was which?

She ran back to Dave and explained the situation.

"We'll have to think of a way to trick the zookeeper into opening the door to Donner's enclosure," Dave said. **"I've got an idea."**

A few minutes later, Holly started to scream. She was good at screaming and she really let rip.

The zookeeper woke with a start and ran out of his hut towards the commotion.

There, in the **ANIMALS OF ASIA** enclosure, he saw a girl hanging by her coat from the antlers of a large reindeer with generous teeth and an eyepatch. The girl, thrashing her arms about and screaming, was being swung from side to side by the reindeer.

The panicked zookeeper ran back into his hut and picked up the phone. He had stayed up late last night celebrating Christmas in the traditional Japanese way: eating KFC. He could be in big trouble if caught sleeping at work. He called the emergency services.

"A girl is being savaged by a reindeer!" he shouted into the phone in Japanese. **"It is terrifying! Help!"**

The startled woman at the other end of the call took down all the details. Soon an ambulance, the fire brigade and the police would be here.

The zookeeper hung up, quickly tidied up all traces of the KFC takeaway lying around, scoured the walls for the key to the **ANIMALS OF ASIA** enclosure, grabbed it and ran back outside. He could see that the reindeer had thrown the girl into a pile of straw at the back of the enclosure and was bellowing at her and stamping its hoof aggressively.

His hands shaking and cursing himself for falling asleep at work, he ran to the door at the back of the enclosure and slipped inside, letting the door close behind him.

Holding his arms out in front of him, he called out to the reindeer, who swung around to face him. It still had the girl's coat hanging from its antlers.

The reindeer lowered its head aggressively. The zookeeper, who was good with animals (naturally, he was a zookeeper), kept speaking softly in Japanese to calm the animal down and it seemed to work.

Talking calmly to the reindeer, the zookeeper managed to move it away from the pile of straw, where the girl must be lying. He shooed it to the other side of the enclosure and ran over to inspect the pile of straw.

There was nothing there but straw.

"Sorry," said a voice in English behind him. **"I didn't mean to upset you, but we had no choice."**

The zookeeper spoke a little English so understood what she said, but he was still confused.

The girl held open the door for the reindeer, retrieving her coat from its antlers as it walked calmly past her and out through the door, then she followed it, closing the door gently behind her.

The zookeeper watched as the girl and the reindeer ran together around to the public side of the enclosure to where some sort of sleigh was parked with another reindeer harnessed to the front of it. The girl and the reindeer jumped into the sleigh, she sat on a big armchair and the reindeer crouched behind; the girl pressed some buttons on a glowing box, then the other reindeer ran a couple of steps forward before taking off into the sky. Within ten seconds they had disappeared from view, heading, it seemed, directly for the moon.

The zookeeper sat down. He needed to take a holiday. He must have been working so hard lately that he was starting to imagine things. He hadn't had a day off all year.

Yes, a holiday. He needed a holiday. A nice holiday to rest. Then he could come back to work refreshed and recovered and he wouldn't imagine flying sleighs or girls and reindeer playing tricks on him.

The distant sound of sirens filled the air.

He would have to think of a story to tell the police and the fire brigade and the ambulance driver. The zookeeper, tired to his bones, lay down right there on the ground, closed his eyes and wondered whether he should have fried chicken for lunch.

CHAPTER TWENTY-ONE

As soon as they took off, Holly got to work on the box.

"It's Dancer next. She's at the top of K2 in Kashmir."

"What's K2?" asked Dave. "I don't remember dropping presents off there."

"We wouldn't have done," said Donner. "No child will ever have set foot there, let alone lived there. It's a mountain, the second-highest mountain in the world and probably the most dangerous."

"Not as dangerous as Mount Everest, surely?"

"Way more dangerous. Dozens of people climb Mount Everest every year – not many have managed to climb K2. The weather can be vicious, and it can change in an instant."

"Well," said Holly, "that's where Dancer is, so let's go and get her."

"Not this time, Holly," said Donner. "You should sit this one out."

"What?! No way! I'm coming."

"Listen, Holly, the temperature at the top of that mountain will be way below freezing. Maybe minus-forty degrees Celsius. You don't have the equipment. People who climb those mountains train for years and have all sorts of special gear – oxygen tanks and special clothes. It would be far too dangerous for you up there."

Holly knew Donner was making a reasonable point and she wasn't being unkind, but something in the way the reindeer spoke to her annoyed Holly. Donner seemed to talk *at* Holly rather than *to* her.

"I think Donner's right," said Dave gently. "We should leave you back at your house. You can look after Comet—"

"What about the magic box?" said Holly. "What happens if I'm not there to operate it? If it clicks out of FLIGHT MODE, then you'll be stuck there. We know that the sleigh keeps me warm, and I can breathe fine when we're way up in the sky in almost space. That's far higher than K2. I'll be all right so long as I don't get out of the sleigh."

The reindeer hesitated.

"And look," said Holly, "the magic box has left rescuing Dancer until after you, so she can't be in major difficulty or it would have had us go there to help her way earlier. Makes sense, no?"

Donner and Dave looked at each other. There was something to be said for this logic.

"You are right," said Donner at last. "We need you to operate the magic box if anything goes wrong. You can come. But you have to promise us that you won't get out of the sleigh, whatever happens. Do you promise?"

What Holly wanted to say to Donner was: "I've just helped rescue Cupid and Comet and Dasher and you, so I don't know why you are treating me like I'm a small child." But she knew that the most important thing right now was finding the next reindeer and doing it as quickly as possible.

"Yes," said Holly, nodding seriously. "I promise."

"Well, then, buckle up," said Donner. "We're heading to one of the most dangerous places on Earth."

CHAPTER TWENTY-TWO

As they sped down towards K2, Donner, Dave and Holly all felt nervous. They knew that the entire success of this trip depended upon one thing: the weather.

If they got lucky, and this was a calm winter's night in the mountains, then their job would be doable.

If they were unlucky and the weather was bad...

This beautiful but savage little corner of

the globe could conjure up some of the most difficult conditions on the planet.

Winds so strong, they could sweep anyone right off the mountain. Temperatures so low that no creature could survive.

And, because the mountain was so high, the air simply didn't have enough oxygen in it to allow people – or reindeer – to breathe for long.

No wonder they were all nervous.

Holly gripped the arms of the chair tightly as the mountains came into view. *The sleigh will protect me*, she thought. It had to.

Holly had seen from the map that they were at the border between China and Pakistan. It was not a part of the world she had given any thought to before. It was amazing to her to realize how big and varied the Earth was and how little she knew of most of it.

It was a dark, clear night in Kashmir. The stars shone magnificently above but even they, for once, were eclipsed by the extraordinary sight of what lay below.

Mountain after mountain stretching off into the distance, each one a thing of wonder in its own right. But the one they were heading towards was something special. It looked like it had been created by an artist, a perfect pyramid, the mountain of all mountains.

Dave and Donner felt it too. They had travelled all over the globe, visiting towns and villages in some of the most remote and extraordinary parts of the world, but even they had never seen anything quite so breathtakingly wonderful.

As they arrowed towards its summit, they could see Dancer. She was lying down,

completely still. Was she all right?

Donner and Dave pulled right up beside her. When she didn't turn to look at them,

Dave nuzzled her gently and said, "Hey there, Dancer, how are you doing?"

Dancer turned around dozily and smiled blearily.

"Hi, Mum," she said. "Is it my birthday?"

"It's me, Dave. Blitzen's replacement? I'm not your mother. You want to get into the sleigh?"

"Will there be cake for my birthday, Mum?" asked Dancer.

"The air is thin up here – it's made her confused," said Donner. "We need to get her into the sleigh, fast."

"How?" asked Dave. "We are all harnessed up. Holly can't get out of the sleigh, it's way too cold."

"She wouldn't be able to lift Dancer into the sleigh anyway," said Donner, sounding worried. "We need a different plan."

Dave turned back to Dancer. **"Do you want some birthday cake, Dancer?"**

Dancer nodded woozily.

"It's in the back of the sleigh. It's lovely cake. Your favourite."

Dancer just laid her head back down in the snow. Dave and Donner looked at each other. This was bad. This was very bad.

Holly had been listening to all this. Encouraging Dancer and reasoning with her clearly wasn't working. They had to try something else. Dancer wasn't herself. It was almost as if they were talking to a tired toddler. Holly tried to imagine what her dad would do if he really wanted her to do something when she was little that was good for her, but she didn't want to do it. She had an idea.

She stood up in the sleigh.

228

"**Dancer!**" she shouted crossly. Dancer's ears pricked up. "**Now you listen to me, young lady. This is your mother speaking. You get up and you get up RIGHT NOW. I will not tolerate this nonsense.**"

Dancer lifted her head off the snow.

"**I said GET UP and come over here,**" said Holly.

Dancer was clearly listening but didn't move. Holly put her hands on her hips.

"**Right, that's it,**" she shouted. "**This is your last chance. I'm going to count to five. If you're not over here in this sleigh by the time I get to five then there will be trouble. Do you understand me, young lady?**"

Dancer nodded.

"**Right, here goes. ONE!**"

Dancer's head flopped back on to the snow.

"I'm **warning you!**" shouted Holly. "**I'm serious! GET UP!**"

Dancer lifted her head back off the snow.

"**TWO!**"

Dancer tried to get to her feet. It was clear this was incredibly difficult for her to do.

"**COME ON!**" Holly yelled as angrily as she could. "**Just do it!**"

Dancer pulled her legs under her and tried to stand.

"**THREE!**"

Dancer strained and strained and eventually staggered to her feet.

"**FOUR! Over here! Come to me!**" shouted Holly, surprised by how fierce she could sound when she wanted to.

The other reindeer looked on in astonishment.

Dancer walked a couple of steps towards the sleigh and then stopped, swaying.

"DON'T YOU DARE!" yelled Holly. **"You're too close to stop now. FOUR AND A HALF!"**

Dancer trudged two more steps. She was now standing next to the sleigh. To Holly's dismay, she began to lean sideways, away from the sleigh.

"DON'T YOU DARE!" repeated Holly. **"DON'T YOU ABSOLUTELY DARE! LEAN THE OTHER WAY OR YOU ARE GROUNDED, YOUNG LADY!"**

Then Holly did what she'd promised the others she wouldn't do: she jumped out of the sleigh and ran round the other side of Dancer.

Instantly, it was almost impossible to breathe. It was like a heavy weight had been placed on her chest.

She could hear the others crying out for her to stop, but she didn't listen. Instead, Holly shoved Dancer as hard as she could. Dancer tottered and ever so slowly fell towards the sleigh, landing inside with a *thud*.

Holly ran back and jumped into the sleigh. She'd been away from the protection of the sleigh for only a few seconds, but she was already dizzy and gasping for breath. She completely understood how Dancer could be in such a state.

"Well done, Holly," she heard Dave say. **"Now, let's get you home."**

With shaking, numb fingers Holly punched the username and password into the magic box, put the sleigh into **FLIGHT MODE** and they were off. Soon one of the world's most beautiful but deadly spots was far behind them.

"I think it's cool. That must have taken a lot of work. Wonder how they get in and out of the house?" said Mr Throat-Badger.

"I suppose it's better than all the lights. I'm going in. It's cold."

"Righto."

The door closed and Holly clambered out of the sleigh. "We made it," she said, her breathing back to normal.

"Just," said Donner severely. "That was quite the risk you took."

"She did it, though," said Dave, smiling at Holly.

Holly got to work unhooking the others. Dancer was still in a bad way, slumped in the bottom of the sleigh.

Dasher came out of the house, bounding up the mountain of presents to the sleigh.

"I was just about to go for a kip, but Comet made me come up here and see if you needed any help," he moaned.

The others went to check on Dancer.

"I don't feel too good," she said as they helped her stand.

"We'll get you inside," said Donner. "Dasher and the Mrs Ditherses will look after you."

"Actually, it's Dorothy Dithers – she's the one with the pink beehive – and Griselda Dithers," said Dasher. "They're all right actually. They made me beans on toast. You want beans on toast, Dancer?"

"Yes please, Daddy," said Dancer, clearly still confused. "I have a ballet class with Dame

Dignity Grunt-Master now, don't I?"

Dasher looked to the others, who shook their heads as if to say *leave it*.

While Donner and Dasher made sure Dancer got inside safely, Holly got to work on the magic box to find the next rescue. They still had to find:

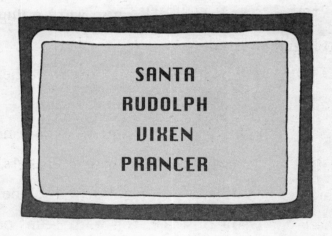

SANTA

RUDOLPH

VIXEN

PRANCER

As well, of course, as Dad.

Holly swallowed. *Dad's got to be with one of the others,* she thought. *He has to be.*

The magic box threw up a surprise this time: *two* reindeer, Vixen and Prancer, in one location.

"That'll help speed things up," said Holly as the Earth spun on the screen. "Do you speak Portuguese?" she said to Dave. He shook his head.

"Shame," said Holly, "because we're going to Brazil."

CHAPTER TWENTY-THREE

It was evening and already dark in Brazil as the sleigh landed in a field as close to the village of Venda das Flores as they dared get.

As Holly stepped out of the sleigh, the warm air hit her like a duvet. She had forgotten that, although Christmas fell in the middle of winter in the Northern Hemisphere, for all the countries below the equator it fell right in the middle of their summer. For the people who lived there, Christmas was associated with good weather and summer holidays. Once again, Holly marvelled at how big Earth was and how little of it she knew.

The village of Venda das Flores was surrounded by countryside and a ring of hills. As they had flown in, Holly noticed one main road running right through the middle of the village and guessed that there were maybe a hundred houses in total.

Perhaps on a normal summer's evening this was a peaceful and relaxing place to be. Not tonight.

Holly and Dave could hear the sound of drums, guitars and people clapping and cheering. There was a big Christmas parade processing down the main road through the village.

"I'm doing this one alone," said Holly. **"There are too many people out there and**

you will stand out and cause problems."

"That means that Vixen and Prancer are standing out too," said Dave. Then he started laughing. "You won't blend in yourself dressed like that, Holly!"

Holly realized she was still dressed in her winter clothes, including beanie hat and gloves.

"Good point!" said Holly. "This will all have to go. I'm boiling."

"Be careful," said Dave.

"I won't be long, I'm sure," said Holly and once she'd shed her coat, hat and gloves, she gave him the thumbs up and ran towards the parade.

Sneaking between two houses, Holly checked out the parade as it passed. There were hundreds of people on the street, all moving in the same direction: men and women, children, a few dogs. A band consisting of about fifteen drummers was making a terrific noise. There were several men playing guitars, but it was difficult to hear the sound they were making over the drums. There was, however, no sign of any reindeer.

Yellow lamps lit up the street, but the real colour came from the costumes being worn by most of the crowd. They were spectacular. Loose fitting shirts and trousers made up of vivid blues and reds and yellows. Many people had garlands of brightly coloured paper flowers around their necks as well as ribbons tied all over their costumes.

The main event though, the most eye-catching part of these outfits, the things Holly could not help but gawk at, were the headdresses and the masks that everyone in costume wore. Some were grotesque – stark white square faces, big unnatural mouths frozen in wild grins, pointed hats from which coloured ribbons cascaded, red and gold hair flowing from the back, golden beards and moustaches. Some masks had bright red faces peppered with little white squares like freckles, others had rows of square teeth, or beards protruding from under the masks.

Other masks were bizarre versions of animals. One looked like a monkey or ape of some kind: big sharp white teeth in an enormous mouth with vivid candy-floss-pink gums; a face of red cheekbones, acid yellow nose, green eyebrows all surrounded with pink fluffy fuzzy hair. One was a rat of some kind: one solitary big upper tooth, pointy nose, massive ears. Noses were long and sharp or squat and squashed. Everything was cartoonish and exaggerated.

And everyone in costume was dancing to the relentless drumming. A jerky, pulsing, rhythmic swaying and twisting and jumping kind of dance. It was hypnotic.

Not everyone was in costume and there were lots of people just walking along, enjoying the music and the spectacle.

Holly scanned the crowd again for Vixen and Prancer. It surely wouldn't be tough to spot them here; they would stand out like a sore thumb. As would Holly. Everyone here probably knew everyone else; it wasn't a big village. How could she blend in?

Of course! A mask. She needed to find a mask. Across the street was a small statue on which someone had placed a mask that looked like a frenzied pirate: a long flowing black beard, wonky eyeholes and a big multi-coloured hat with bright green hair sprouting out underneath.

Holly darted over, snatched the mask off the statue, plonked it on her head and, before anyone noticed or said anything, she shuffled back into the middle of the parade. Soon she was dancing and clapping with the rest of the colourful crowd. All the while she looked out through the small eyeholes for a clue as to where Vixen and Prancer might be.

It wasn't long before she'd skipped and danced her way to the front of the parade and saw that it was heading into a small town square. There were strings of coloured lights slung from building to building. One side was dominated by a big church, easily the largest building in the town. In front of the church was a Nativity scene: a manger, straw on the ground, an electric star shining above, even a stuffed sheep to one side. No Jesus, Mary or Joseph, though.

On another side was a café, lit inside by fluorescent lights. A few old men sat outside at tables, smoking and drinking coffee.

The parade entered the square and it seemed like this was where it would end. The drummers gathered in one corner, still playing loudly and cheerfully, and the square began to fill with laughing, dancing villagers. But Vixen and Prancer were nowhere to be seen.

At last, the drumming and the singing stopped for a moment and was replaced by shouts and clapping as the last of the parade entered the square. Two clowns on stilts leading someone dressed, Holly assumed, as a heavily pregnant Mary and another dressed as

Joseph. And Mary and Joseph were sitting, not as tradition on donkeys, but … on two reindeer. Vixen and Prancer!

The crowd cheered the arrival of Mary and Joseph and parted to let the clowns lead the reindeer through the square and over to the Nativity scene in front of the church.

That solves the problem of where the reindeer are, thought Holly. And replaced it with another problem: how to get them out of here as quickly and quietly as possible?

The crowd surged in behind the reindeer as they reached the front of the church. The clowns twirled and hopped from side to side, then helped Mary and Joseph slide off the backs of the reindeer. Mary lay down in the straw and Joseph sat on a small stool beside her. A bemused-looking Vixen and Prancer were led to the back of the scene and encouraged to eat hay from a trough.

The clowns then started singing a song with which the rest of the crowd joined in as a priest pushed through the throng of people and started to throw holy water at Mary, Joseph and the reindeer.

Holly pushed and shoved her way to the front and stood there in her mask trying to work out how to handle this. She couldn't just go up and grab the reindeer, could she? And she certainly couldn't explain the whole story, even if she could speak Portuguese. She could wait until the square emptied and everyone went home – but that could take hours and Holly didn't have hours.

The priest was saying prayers over Mary and Joseph, and the people in the square were joining in.

After perhaps twenty minutes, the priest finished and held up his hands with a broad grin on his face. This drew a cheer from the crowd and as the drummers started up again people resumed their dancing and singing.

Holly figured this was her chance to act. She had to get to Vixen and Prancer first and explain the situation.

Pretending to dance she sashayed over to the first reindeer.

"Hello!" she said as loudly as she dared. The reindeer looked at her.

"I'm Holly," she continued. **"You don't know me but…"**

Before she could say any more, there was a piercing scream from a girl close by. She was about Holly's age, and she pointed aggressively at Holly and yelled something Holly couldn't understand to a group of women standing with her. Then she pointed back down the route the parade had come from.

"Maria! Maria! O que está acontecendo?" one

249

of the women said.

The girl, Maria, shouted at Holly again.

What was going on?

The women looked disapprovingly at Holly. Had they worked out that Holly was an imposter trying to take the reindeer? Maria stomped over to Holly and started to shout at her, face to face.

Holly smiled as warmly as she could but then remembered she was wearing a mask.

The mask! The mask probably belonged to Maria! Maybe she had made it and now she was upset with Holly for stealing it. That must be it!

What could Holly do? Take it off and give it back? That would reveal her as a complete stranger. But if she refused to give back the mask then there would be trouble. Either way

Holly would receive a lot of unwanted attention.

Before she could decide, Maria lunged at Holly and tried to wrench the mask off her head. Holly clung on.

Then the fireworks began. Not a display off in the distance but just a few metres away. *BANG! POP!* The sound was deafening as they exploded dangerously close by. The reindeer began bucking and barking in alarm.

Sensing an opportunity in the chaos, Holly let go of the mask and Maria, still pulling hard, lost her balance and fell backwards, mask in hand.

Holly spun round to the reindeer. **"Are you Vixen?"**

The startled reindeer nodded.

"OK, Vixen, so that means the other reindeer is Prancer. Can't explain now but I've

come to rescue you!"

Vixen nodded again.

Meanwhile, Maria had got back to her feet. She pointed at Holly and shouted, **"LADRA! LADRA!"**

Holly assumed this meant "thief", so having it shouted at her while she *was* trying to steal a reindeer was not helpful.

The drummers drummed, fireworks exploded, Maria shouted: it was *chaos*. Holly decided that there was no talking her way out of this one even if she wanted to. It was time to leave if she was going to save Christmas and Dad.

She untied Vixen and Prancer and ran with them up the steps towards the open church door. Maria followed. And so did fifty villagers. At the top of the steps, Holly jumped on to Vixen's back.

A big burly man lunged to try to grab the rope tied around Vixen's neck but just missed. Holly urged the animal forward and into the church. Prancer followed.

Galloping down the aisle, Holly spotted an open door on the right.

"Turn right, Vixen! Look! A way out!"

Vixen and Prancer attempted to turn, but the floor of the church was covered in shiny tiles that their hooves couldn't grip. Instead, both reindeer slid sideways ten metres straight up the aisle, stopping just before the altar.

Turning around, they started back down the aisle as a large group of villagers advanced towards them. Trying to turn, left this time, proved just as difficult as before, and once again Vixen and Prancer skidded on their knees, sliding right at the oncoming villagers.

The locals, not wanting to be flattened, leapt out of the way. The reindeer slid past, continuing right through the church door and back into the square.

Holly decided her only option was back through the square and down the route of the parade.

Blocking her way was Maria, her face contorted in fury, defiantly holding out a palm to say, **"Stop!"**

Holly couldn't stop even if she tried; she was heading right at Maria at full speed. She pulled back on Vixen's neck, shouting, **"JUMP!!!"**

They soared off the top step of the church and high into the air, over an astonished Maria, landing with a thud on the other side.

Holly came so close to falling off, but she managed to cling on.

As they landed, a firework went off right by Holly's ear and this made both her and Vixen lurch to the right, almost wiping out the clown on stilts.

Vixen's antlers connected with the multi-coloured outfit the clown was wearing, ripping it completely off in one motion. Vixen and Prancer bolted off down the main road and, with the clown's clothes flapping from Vixen's antlers, Holly turned to see receding into the distance a stunned Maria standing with her mouth open and a clown on stilts wearing nothing but his underpants.

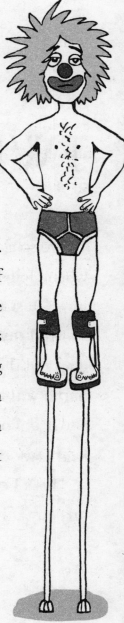

CHAPTER TWENTY-FOUR

"We're so close to getting this done," said Dave when Holly brought Vixen and Prancer back to him. "Just Rudolph and Santa to go."

"And my dad," Holly reminded him, as she checked the magic box. "Do you really think Santa will know where he is?"

"If anyone can find him, it will be Santa," said Dave confidently.

"Let's hope so. I've got a lock on Rudolph anyway," Holly said. "The magic box is showing me where he is. Let's go straight there, shall we?"

"Will we have time? We haven't been to your house so time might not reset."

"We'll be fine," said Holly. "I want to get on with it. I have to find my dad. I'm so worried about him."

Holly settled back in the armchair as they took off. And boy did they take off! The sleigh was now being pulled by Dave, Vixen and Prancer and their combined power was extraordinary. As Holly was forcibly pinned back into the seat, she could only imagine what it felt like for the sleigh to fly with the full complement of reindeer.

Holly tried to push away thoughts of her dad. He was safe – he had to be. Santa would help when they found him. She could only control the things she could control, and right now there was a job to do. They were flying to Las Vegas because that was where Rudolph was.

Las Vegas is situated in the Mojave Desert in the south-western corner of the USA. Just down the road is Death Valley, famous for being the place where the highest temperature on Earth was once recorded: fifty-six point seven degrees Celsius.

Death Valley is a tough place to visit. It's not called Death Valley for nothing. It's the driest place on the planet. If you enjoy rain, or any water, it isn't for you. So, you could be forgiven for thinking that its neighbour, Las Vegas, might be equally as bleak and harsh. But that

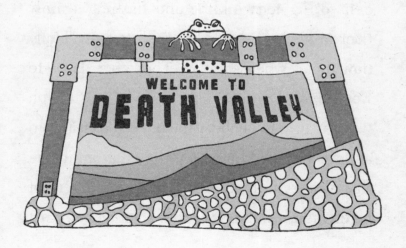

isn't the case. Las Vegas is a busy, bustling, modern city plonked right down in the middle of the desert.

As Holly saw the city come into view, she couldn't help but feel it was kind of beautiful. Not beautiful in the way a mountain is beautiful or a river is beautiful, but beautiful in a different way. From the air, with the sun beginning to set and with a warm toasty orange glow flooding the desert, Las Vegas was an oasis of light, twinkling and flashing against the darkening sky. The first person Holly thought of when she saw it was her dad. He would have *loved* it.

Las Vegas is a holiday town. People visit from all over the world to enjoy the entertainments that it offers and there are dozens and dozens of hotels offering all sorts of shows: famous singers, famous comedians, famous magicians and lots more besides. What mischief was Rudolph getting up to? Nothing would surprise the other reindeer. Rudolph was great at pulling the sleigh, but he also loved being the centre of attention. If there was anywhere he would shine, it would be here.

The box told them that Rudolph was in the Golden Cornflake Hotel, one of the biggest hotels in the city. It had a vast car park, and they took a gamble by landing in the far corner of it. They came in as steeply as possible, almost vertically, then swerved at the last moment, hit the brakes and screeched to a halt behind a coach.

Dave thought that Las Vegas, like New York, was the kind of place where three reindeer pulling a sleigh would not look particularly out of place, but they decided to play it safe – Holly would go and see what she could find, and the reindeer would stand by in case of emergency. Vixen had warned Holly that deserts could get very cold at night, so she had her warm clothes on again. She jumped off the sleigh and headed across the car park towards the hotel.

At the entrance, a man dressed as a giant cornflake opened the door for her.

"Welcome back to the Golden Cornflake, young lady," he said with a big smile on his face. **"You have a good evening now."**

Holly smiled and nodded her head.

Walking into the lobby of the Golden Cornflake was like entering a different world. On the left was the reception desk, on the right the Concierge and, beyond, row after row after row of fruit machines with people sitting in front of them gambling.

Holly walked through and noticed a glazed look on all the faces of those playing. They looked like zombies, their pale unresponsive expressions lit up by the colourful flashing lights of the machines, as they pressed buttons, waited, pressed buttons, waited. On and on.

Even winning money didn't seem to provoke any response. *How long have they been here?* Holly wondered. It wouldn't have surprised her if they had been there for hours. They seemed sort of brainwashed.

Beyond the fruit machines there was a casino, dozens of tables where people were playing cards and other games. As she stood staring at it, a man approached Holly. He too was dressed as giant golden cornflake.

"Good evening, young lady. This is an area for the over-twenty-ones only! I must ask you to return to the family areas."

"Oh, **of course,**" said Holly as confidently as she could. **"What I'm looking for is … the reindeer. Do you know where the reindeer is?"**

"I'm sorry," said the giant cornflake. **"Did you say the reindeer?"**

"Yes," said Holly, "reindeer. I was told you had a reindeer here."

Holly had been told no such thing, of course, but she knew Rudolph was in the building somewhere and she thought it was worth a shot. To her surprise, the cornflake looked around, then leant towards Holly.

"How did you know about the reindeer?" he asked.

Holly shrugged casually. "I just heard," she said.

"It's supposed to be a secret but, yes, we've got a reindeer appearing on the Big Cornflake Stage in twenty minutes. He just showed up at a rehearsal earlier, walked up to the microphone and started singing. It was incredible. Must be some sort of trick but it's impressive. You have a ticket?"

"Can you get me one?" asked Holly.

"No, but I'm going to be on the door. I'll get you in if you like."

"That," said Holly, "would be amazing."

Holly had no money to buy a drink, so she sat in the seat she'd been shown to and waited.

The performance opened with a woman in a sparkly full-length dress coming on and singing a noisy song that seemed to be about showbusiness. It was all about how tough it was to be a singer but how it was the best thing in the world.

Make up your mind, thought Holly. *Which one is it?*

The woman had the biggest smile and the whitest teeth that Holly had ever seen. At the end of the song she shouted, "Thank you!" about twenty times and bowed a lot. Then she said, **"It is my greatest pleasure to introduce to you the best chorus line in Las Vegas. It's BETTY BOWL and the FANTASTIC FLAKES!!!!"**

The curtain behind her opened, revealing a grand sweeping staircase down which a large white bowl with two stockinged legs sticking out the bottom was dancing. She high-kicked her way down the stairs as the band played some frantic music. Holly wondered how the bowl-woman could see where she was going. There must be some kind of panel in the side of the bowl that she was looking through.

Then, from the side of the stage, ran on twenty men dressed as cornflakes.

They all danced around the bowl, creating intricate patterns and singing about spoons.

Suddenly, the bowl-woman shrieked, **"Oh no! It's the Cocoa Nuggets!"** and from the other side of the stage twelve men and women dressed as giant chocolate rice balls ran on and everyone on stage started fake-fighting except for the bowl-woman who ran around singing about how difficult it was to be so good-looking and have everyone fighting over you.

Eventually the Cocoa Nuggets, who were clearly the bad guys, were repulsed by the Fantastic Flakes and the bowl-woman sang a love song while the giant cornflakes ran up the stairs and dived off the top into the bowl. Although that must have been an optical illusion, thought Holly, because there was no way that bowl could take the weight of all those men dressed as cornflakes.

At the end, the audience went wild. The

woman sat next to Holly was crying so hard that Holly thought she must have just received some bad news, but it turned out she was just really moved by the show.

The original woman in the sparkly dress came on stage again and smiled her massive toothy smile. **"Betty Bowl and the Fantastic Flakes!"** she said. **"They'll be back later with their smash hit 'Dairy, Oat or Soy – it's All Just Milk to Me'."** There was a round of applause and the woman next to Holly started crying again.

"Now then, we have a new act for your pleasure and it's going to blow your minds. It's Rudolph the Singing Reindeer!"

All the lights went out, the curtain at the back of the stage opened and a spotlight picked out a smiling Rudolph in a tuxedo. He sashayed down to the front of the stage as the band

began to play a number. The audience bubbled
with excitement again.

Oh no, thought Holly. If Rudolph started
singing it would cause a sensation and word
would spread like wildfire.

It was incredibly selfish
and reckless of Rudolph to
even consider doing this,
but Holly could already
see how hungry he was
for fame and attention.
He was loving the
audience's reaction and
blew kisses at some of the
women in the front row.

Holly had to act. And quickly. She could see the introduction to the song was nearly over and Rudolph was preparing to sing.

Holly leapt from her seat and ran down to the stage. To Rudolph's surprise and annoyance, she signalled for the band to stop playing. After a moment, they did.

Rudolph stepped angrily towards her, and Holly whispered in his ear, **"Santa is outside and he is not happy. So I'd be quiet and listen if I were you."**

This clearly unsettled Rudolph, who took a couple of steps backwards.

"Hi, everyone!" Holly said into the microphone. **"My name is Holly and I'm sorry to disturb this performance, but there's something I need to tell you."**

The crowd began murmuring; they

clearly did not appreciate having this show interrupted.

"I'm from **Great Britain**," said Holly. "I've come a long way. And ... and I have something to tell you about Rudolph here..."

Holly trailed off. She had no idea what to say. The eyes of everyone in the room were on her. She looked at the crying woman and had an idea.

"Um ... it's a sad story. You see, Rudolph ... was abandoned as a young reindeer."

Someone in the audience gasped.

"Yes, abandoned!" continued Holly. "After he was born, his mother ran off to join the circus and his dad ran off to join ... another different circus. Rudolph had no one. I found him wandering the streets and took him in and raised him as a brother. It was always Rudolph's dream to sing in Las Vegas, but Rudolph's a reindeer and of course he can't sing. Or get on a plane to Las Vegas. No airlines allow reindeer on their planes. Have you ever seen a reindeer on a plane?"

Some members of the audience shook their heads.

"Exactly! That's what he was up against! He had a dream and I wanted to help make his dream come true. So I saved all my pocket money for ten years and bought him a ticket to Las Vegas and persuaded the airline to take him, just so he could have this special moment because it was always his dream. To stand up here and pretend to sing. I'll take him home now. But thank you! Thank you! Thank you for helping this poor reindeer realize his dream! We all have dreams! Keep dreaming! Bye! Be the best you can be! Have a great night!"

The audience looked confused, but a few of them clapped a bit as Holly grabbed Rudolph by the lapels of his tuxedo and led him off the stage towards the exit.

The spangly dress woman came running out, and as Holly and Rudolph broke into a run, they heard her say, **"Awesome! Next we have an Indian Juggler! She's the Thrower from Goa, please welcome Flipping Ada!"**

Rudolph was furious when they got back to the sleigh in the car park to find no Santa.

"You lied to me!" he shouted at Holly.

"Rudolph!" warned Vixen. **"You know full well that Santa would hit the roof if he found out you tried to sing in front of people, so I suggest you let Holly hook you up and we get this sleigh back to her house as quickly as**

possible. You should thank her for not letting you blow it. We haven't been able to deliver the presents and Santa is missing. Christmas is in danger of being cancelled. Do you want to be responsible for that?"

Rudolph said nothing but snorted angrily as Holly tied the straps on his harness. She put the sleigh into **FLIGHT MODE** and Rudolph led the others off with such startling speed that Holly was thrown back into her seat. The sleigh took off almost vertically, leaving Las Vegas rapidly behind.

Holly had been so focused on retrieving Rudolph that she had no idea how much time had passed since she'd last been home. With a sickening lurch she remembered: they had travelled straight from Brazil to Las Vegas. They had been on *two* rescue missions since last being at the house.

Had they been gone too long? Would the sun have risen? Had they blown it?

CHAPTER
TWENTY-FIVE

Within minutes they plummeted towards Holly's house, but this time something was different. It took Holly a moment or two to process what it was.

The sun was coming up; it was getting light.

Holly's heart leapt into her mouth.

As they hurtled down, Dave turned to look at her. There was a desperate look in his eyes. Holly could hardly stand it. Were they really out of time? Was Christmas ruined?

No, wait! thought Holly. *The sun hasn't hit our roof yet. Not quite. As soon as we land, time will jump back and the Throat-Badgers will drive up in their car and talk about Dad's decorations and it'll all be fine. We just cut it a bit too close this time. We won't make that mistake again.*

The sleigh screeched to a halt in its usual place on the mound of presents. Holly waited

for the sky to darken. For time to jump back.
For everything to be all right.

Nothing happened.

Nothing.

At the top of the mound of presents, at
the highest point of the pile, was one present
beautifully wrapped in shiny gold paper and
it suddenly blazed as the dawn sunlight hit it. It

was so bright that Holly, Rudolph, Dave, Vixen and Prancer all turned to look.

No one spoke, the only sound was the heavy breathing of the reindeer after the exertions of their journey from Las Vegas. There was no need to speak; everyone knew what was happening.

After a couple of seconds, sunlight hit the present below the gold one, creeping down the stack towards the roof.

Dave was the first to react. **"We need to do something!"** he said.

"Yes, but what?" said Holly.

"I'm the senior reindeer here," said Rudolph. **"I'll give the orders, thank you."**

"Fine," said Vixen, her eyes fixed on the light travelling down the stack of presents. **"What are your orders? Because I think we**

have about thirty seconds before the sunlight reaches Holly's roof!"

"OK! OK!" shouted Rudolph. "Don't rush me!"

There was a pause while they all waited anxiously for Rudolph's plan.

"OK, listen," he said, then trailed off.

"YES?!" said Vixen.

"I…" said Rudolph.

The others leant in to hear his plan.

"I…" he repeated.

Holly was clenching her fists so tightly it hurt.

"I … can't think of anything," said Rudolph.

"For the love of Santa!" Vixen barked angrily.

"We should check the magic box to see where Santa is," suggested Prancer.

"No time! No time to find him and bring him back even if we got a lock on his position," said Dave, also with his eyes fixed on the sunlight making its unstoppable way down the stack towards Holly's roof.

Holly flipped open the lid of the box.

"Seriously, Holly," said Dave. "There's no time!"

"I know!" Holly shouted back. "But there might be something else I can do. Surely the box is our only hope."

"Wait!" yelled Rudolph. "I've thought of something!"

The others all turned to him expectantly. Rudolph stared back at them.

"Well?" said Prancer after a moment. "What's your idea?"

"I've forgotten again," said Rudolph. Vixen

282

tossed her head in exasperation.

Meanwhile, Holly was logging in as quickly as she could, typing SANTA1 then XMAS_BIG_BOY.

The sunlight crept closer and closer to the roof.

"Let's ask Santa," said Rudolph.

"WE DON'T KNOW WHERE HE IS!" shouted Vixen.

"Oh yeah," said Rudolph, adding, "I'm still the senior reindeer."

"You're certainly the senior fool!" retorted Vixen.

"Why, you—"

"STOP IT!" yelled Dave, surprising himself with his boldness. He would *never* normally speak to senior reindeer in this way. "BOTH OF YOU! WE NEED TO GIVE HOLLY A CHANCE TO

DO SOMETHING!"

Holly continued to ignore all this and focused on the box. She scrolled through the screens looking for something, anything, that might help. Nothing obvious jumped out at her.

Prancer was watching the sunlight creeping down towards the roof. **"I think we have about five seconds,"** he said.

Suddenly all were quiet. This situation had never arisen before. If Christmas was cancelled ... well, then what? What would happen to the reindeer? To the sleigh? To Santa?

The sun was about to reach the roof; they all held their breath. Holly hit something on the screen and the magic box pulsed and turned black. There was a low boom, a shock wave rippled out from the magic box and

Holly braced herself for the worst.

When she dared open her eyes again, she could not believe what she saw.

CHAPTER TWENTY-SIX

All was still. Very still. The reindeer stood like statues. Were they frozen? Were they ... dead?

Holly jumped down from the sleigh and rushed over to Dave.

He had his eyes open. He didn't look dead: his eyes were bright; he was warm to the touch.

The other reindeer were in exactly the same state.

Holly looked around and saw something else which astonished her so much she nearly fell off the stack of presents: a blackbird over the house next door was suspended in mid-air. Just hanging there, its wings outstretched.

The whole scene reminded Holly of a photograph: a moment frozen in time. But it wasn't a photograph, it was her street, her house, her reindeer friends, and she could move among them.

That's it! she said to herself. *I've frozen time! Or rather the box has.*

Holly quickly climbed down the huge pile of presents to the ground and rushed into her house.

A part of her was hoping to find Santa or her dad or someone to help her work out what to do. All throughout this adventure, she'd had Dave by her side. Now she was alone, and she didn't like it.

In the living room she found Comet and Dasher: both frozen like the others. In the kitchen were Dancer, Donner and Cupid, frozen too.

Holly ran upstairs, checked all the bedrooms and the bathroom. There was no one there.

Downstairs again, she realized there was no way out into the back garden – the pile of presents blocked the way. Running out into the front garden, dizzy with panic, she bumped into Mrs Dithers and Mrs Dithers coming back down the path towards her.

She was not sure what shocked her the most: that they, like her, were still able to walk around with the rest of the world frozen in time or that neither of them was wearing a wig or, perhaps most extraordinarily, that both of them were dressed in a skirt and cardigan and *not* their white lacy dresses.

In fact, they looked so different, so odd, that it took Holly a second to realize who they were.

"Hello, Mrs Dithers," Holly said. "And hello, other Mrs Dithers. We have a problem."

Standing in the hallway because there was no room elsewhere – the kitchen and living room being full of large motionless reindeer – Holly explained to Mrs Dithers and Mrs Dithers what had happened as clearly as she could. Having to say it all out loud, it sounded bonkers, but they seemed to accept it without question.

"So that's the story," said Holly. "What do you think we should do?"

Dorothy Dithers and Griselda Dithers turned to look at each other and then back to Holly.

"No idea," said Dorothy.

"Not a clue," said Griselda.

Holly's heart sank. **"There must be a reason why everyone else has been frozen in time and the three of us haven't,"** she said. **"Why would that be?"**

Dorothy and Griselda shrugged.

"Do you have any idea where Santa might be?" persisted Holly. **"Or my dad?"**

Dorothy and Griselda shook their heads.

"None at all?"

"None," said Dorothy.

"Not a clue," said Griselda.

Holly sighed. She walked back through the front door to see what was happening out there. The reindeer hadn't moved. She looked to the blackbird: it too seemed to be in the same position ... except ... something was different about it.

Yes! Its wings were in a slightly different

position. It *was* still moving, just incredibly slowly. So time hadn't stopped, it had just slowed right down.

Which meant the sun would still be rising and at some point, it would hit Holly's roof.

She panicked. She ran across the road and looked in through the window of the Throat-Badgers' kitchen. Mr Throat-Badger was there in his dressing gown at the sink filling the kettle – his body still, the water coming out of the tap seemingly motionless.

Holly ran to the side of the Throat-Badgers' garden and looked over their fence. Big Bad Wolf, their German Shepherd, was suspended in motion halfway across the lawn.

She ran back inside her own house. **"Come on!"** she said to the two Mrs Ditherses. **"We have to work this out before the sun hits our** roof. Why have the three of us been allowed to move normally? It must mean that between us we hold the answer. We just have to think what it is."

"We have been thinking actually," said Dorothy.

"And?" asked Holly. "What's the answer? Why haven't we been frozen?"

"Couldn't think of anything to do with that," said Griselda. "Sorry. We meant we were thinking about what we chatted to the reindeer about while you were gone."

Holly put her head in her hands. "Go on," she said. "We haven't got any other clues so tell me."

"They were asking about our white lacy dresses," said Dorothy.

"We both always wore the same dress,"

said Griselda.

"We've worn nothing else for years," said Dorothy. "And they wanted to know why."

"Sure," said Holly. "I kind of want to know that too."

"Well," began Dorothy, "Griselda and I are twins and have lived next door for our whole lives."

"And that's a *long* time now," said Griselda.

"Anyway," continued Dorothy, "many years ago, we met Horace and Graham. They were twins too. I fell in love with Horace and Griselda fell in love with Graham. They asked us to marry them, and we both said yes. We decided to have a joint wedding. On the day of the wedding, Griselda and I walked down the aisle together in these beautiful white lacy dresses. It was the happiest moment of our lives."

"A choir sang, the church was full of flowers, it was so beautiful," said Griselda.

"But Horace and Graham weren't there," said Dorothy. "They just … weren't there. We waited at the church for hours. We knew they'd show up eventually."

"But they didn't."

"Then we came home and waited for them here. We've been waiting ever since."

"It's been nearly seventy years and no sign of them," said Griselda. "Since then, one of us has always sat in the window looking at the road so we wouldn't miss them when they came back."

"Because they would come back," said Dorothy. "Of that we were certain."

"We were telling the reindeer that story

tonight and we realized something. Horace and Graham are not coming back."

That took you seventy years to realize? thought Holly.

"I know that sounds bizarre," said Dorothy. "But let me tell you, it's easier to hold on to the hope that they're coming back rather than face up to the pain that they're not."

"Yes," said Griselda.

"We were stuck."

"We were."

"I still love Horace, though."

"And I still love Graham."

"One day we'll find out what happened to them, but we've been trapped, trapped in our grief, and it's time to leave it behind us and move on."

"We have to move on."

"So just now we took the dresses off and put on something else."

"It's time to move on."

There was a pause. Holly didn't know what to say.

"Such a sad story," she said. "And quite … strange. Hope you don't mind me saying that."

Dorothy and Griselda shrugged.

"But I guess," said Holly slowly, "we all have things that happened a long time ago that still bother us."

Dorothy and Griselda nodded.

"I suppose Dad found it hard after Mum died," Holly continued. "He's hung on to that. She loved Christmas, so we love Christmas. She liked Christmas lights, so Dad gets more and more lights every year."

Dorothy and Griselda nodded again.

"He won't let me open this trunk of her letters in the attic," said Holly. "He's still not moved on in some ways. That's a bit like you and your dresses – he's clinging on to the past. Trapped by it."

Dorothy and Griselda said, very gently, "We know."

"Everyone gets stuck sometimes," said Dorothy. "They need someone to come and find them. You rescued all those reindeer, didn't you?"

"With Dave's help," said Holly loyally.

"Well, you found them and saved them. I'm sure you'll find your dad and Santa too."

"Wait a minute," said Holly after a moment. "What if ... what if Dad and Santa are trapped somewhere too?"

"Now you're talking! Where could Santa be

trapped?" said Dorothy.

"Up a chimney?" Griselda laughed.

They stood for a beat looking at each other. Then, all having the same thought at the same time, ran down the hallway, into the living room and over to the fireplace. Holly leant over and looked up the chimney. It was dark, too

dark to see anything.

"Santa?" she said, feeling a little foolish. "Are you there?"

There was no reply.

"My name is Holly," she continued, "and I'm here with some of your reindeer. Dave is probably the one I know best, but he's frozen, and time seems to have slowed down because I pushed a button on your magic box and—"

"Which button?" It was a man's voice. A deep, rumbling man's voice and it was coming from the chimney.

"Santa? Is it really you?" Holly's voice quivered.

"It's really me. I didn't want to give myself away, but if you know about Dave and the magic box ... well. I seem to be stuck in this chimney. Can you pull me down please?"

Holly reached up into the darkness, but however hard she stretched, she couldn't quite get far enough up.

"I can't get to you, Santa," she said. "We need my dad, I think."

"Will you go and get him please?"

"I'll try," said Holly. "I have an idea. Hold on."

She turned and ran out of the room and up the stairs. Santa had been trapped up the chimney, and if her dad was trapped too there was only one place that could be.

Sliding the attic ladder down, she climbed up and into the loft. Her heart thumped in her chest. If her dad wasn't where she thought he might be, then they were in trouble. Even though time was slowed down, it hadn't completely stopped. The sunlight couldn't be far from hitting the roof by now. Maybe they

were already too late?

She found The Trunk and with shaking hands undid the lock. Her whole life she had wanted to look inside this trunk. The latch slid open, she lifted the lid and there, with barely enough room, curled up into a tight ball, was her father.

CHAPTER TWENTY-SEVEN

Her dad removed Santa from the chimney, which was no easy task as his belt had caught on a hook halfway up. It involved huge effort from Simon and a not inconsiderable amount of pain inflicted on Santa. After that, everything else was accomplished quickly.

Santa climbed the stack of presents in no time at all; he really was in great shape.

Logging on to his account on the magic box, after getting Holly to remind him of his password, he dealt with everything in seconds. He managed to jump time back to the arrival home of the Throat-Badgers.

"Thierry! I forbid you to like it! It's naff, naff, *naff*!"

Reindeer back in their right positions, presents back in the hold, it was time to get on; they had gifts to deliver.

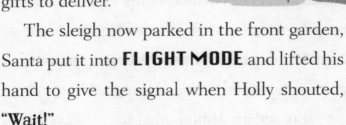

The sleigh now parked in the front garden, Santa put it into **FLIGHT MODE** and lifted his hand to give the signal when Holly shouted, **"Wait!"**

Santa, not used to being given orders in this way, raised his eyebrows in surprise.

Holly ran over to Dave and threw her arms around him.

"We did it!" she whispered. "You're amazing!"

Dave, worried he'd burst into tears if he spoke, said nothing.

Holly didn't want to let go. Rudolph, annoyed that he wasn't the centre of attention, tossed his head arrogantly.

"Hurry up!" he said after a while. "Or I'll fart again."

Holly finally let go of Dave's neck, stood back, wiped away a tear and watched as Santa and his reindeer took off into the night sky, off to make sure that every child got the present they deserved.

"You did it, Holly," said Dad. "You saved Christmas. You and Dave."

Holly looked up at him. "Dad, I know we all love Christmas," she said carefully. "I know Mum did too. Christmas is the best. But Mum wouldn't want us to live in the past. Or to be afraid of it."

Dad put his arm around her. "I see that now, Holly. Perhaps we can open up The Trunk later?"

She nodded. "I'd like that."

"I still like Christmas lights, though," he said. "The brighter the better, I say!"

Walking arm in arm with her father back into the house, Holly was astounded to see that there, in the living room, in front of the Christmas tree, with a big ribbon around its neck, stood a pony. Attached to its bridle was a tag that read:

MERRY CHRISTMAS, HOLLY.
WITH LOVE FROM SANTA
(AND DAVE) xxxx

THE GREAT REINDEER RESCUE

⭐2

⭐5

⭐4

⭐3 TAHITI ⭐4 TOKYO, JAPAN

FLORES, BRAZIL ⭐7 LAS VEGAS, USA

ACKNOWLEDGEMENTS

Once again Anita has done a wonderful job with the illustrations. Thanks, sis. Lauren Fortune, my editor, has guided me and encouraged me with great grace. Thanks too to Sarah Dutton, Aimee Stewart and everyone at Scholastic who worked so hard to get this book into shape. Thanks to Penelope Daukes, who is so brilliant at getting the word out there and does it with such joy. Thanks to Genevieve Herr for her book savviness. Thanks as always to Peter Nixon for his support and encouragement and to Paul Stevens for his expert guidance. And, last but not least, thanks to Louise who makes my world go round.

DON'T MISS:

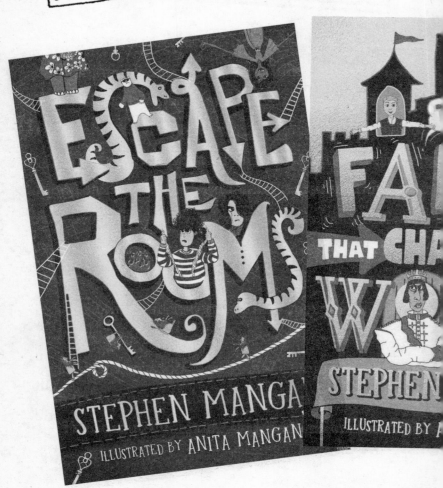